M000034560

PEDESTAL

BY

ASHLEY SARGEANT HAGAN

INKWELL
LITERARY PRESS

Nashville, TN

INKWELL
LITERARY PRESS

Inkwell Literary Press
Nashville, TN

Copyright © Ashley Sargeant Hagan, 2017
All Rights Reserved
Printed in the United States of America

ISBN: 978-0-69285-988-9 (paperback)
ISBN: 978-0-69289-702-7 (ebook)

Without limiting the rights under copyright reserved above, no part
of this publication may be reproduced, stored in or introduced into a
retrieval system, or transmitted, in any form, or by any means
(electronic, mechanical, photocopying, recording, or otherwise),
without the prior written permission of both the copyright owner
and the above publisher of this book.

This is a work of fiction. Names, characters, places, and incidents either
are the product of the author's imagination or are used fictitiously,
and any resemblance to actual persons, living or dead, business
establishments, events, or locales is entirely coincidental.

The publisher does not have any control over and does not assume any
responsibility for author or third-party Web sites or their content.

The scanning, uploading, and distribution of this book via the Internet
or via any other means without the permission of the publisher is illegal
and punishable by law. Please purchase only authorized electronic
editions, and do not participate in or encourage electronic piracy of
copyrighted materials. Your support of the author's rights is appreciated.

Cover design by Pat Evans and Sarah Siegand. Cover illustration by
Pugovica88/Shutterstock. Interior design by Sarah Siegand. Headshot
photography by Jon Alan Salon, Nashville, TN.

To Agatha Christie

PRONUNCIATION
DICTIONARY

TURKISH

- **Kara Inci** *(*kə'-rə een'-chee) — black pearl

- **Çırağan Palace Hotel** (tseer' ən) — a former Ottoman residence and now a hotel

- **Cannakkale** (kən' ə kəl) — a province in Turkey

- **Kirikkale** (keer' ə kəl) — a province in Turkey

- **Eleni** (eh len' ee) — Helen

- **Eleni tis Troias** (eh len' ee tees troy' əs) — Helen of Troy

ARABIC

- **inayyi** (in ə' yee) — light of my eyes

1

Bleary-eyed, Edwin Sterling fumbled with his phone. He came to an abrupt halt in the terminal, causing his leather rolling carry-on bag to knock against the leg of his well-fitted suit. He pressed the phone to his ear as he closed his blue eyes against the day.

"It's way too early in the morning. I should still be in bed," he grumbled good-naturedly into the phone without so much as a hello.

"What time is it there?" asked his assistant, unfazed by her employer's greeting. Jen Murphy was an Irish red-head, attractively freckled from head to toe, who was used to her boss' temperamental ways.

Edwin glanced down at his phone.

"Seven twenty-three. Fifty-two minutes until my flight. And I can't get back to London too soon."

"Oh, Edwin," Jen remonstrated. "Was the gala that bad? You usually like doing these charity events."

"It was fine," he sighed apologetically, running his free hand through his hair and obliterating the order that his light brown curls had started the morning with. "I'm just not used to being alone at these things. It makes me feel very exposed. There were at least two very wealthy, big-haired American women ready to become Mrs. Sterling at a moment's notice. Promise you won't get sick again. It was very unkind of you. If you're going to remain my assistant, I need you to stay well."

"I promise," Jen laughed. "Sorry it was such an ordeal."

"Oh, well. All in the name of cancer research," said Edwin in a martyred voice and gazing into the middle distance as if he had an audience.

"So, I have Bill picking you up at Heathrow this evening. That way you don't have to take a cab. Hopefully there won't be a swarm of fans."

"Thanks. By the way, I do hope you're feeling better."

"Yes, I'm on the mend," said Jen. "Gerald is taking good care of me. I don't know if he quite realized last August that 'for better or for worse' included the stomach flu, though."

"Oh, married life," Edwin complained. "I believe you're bragging again."

"I'm not," she giggled. "Just you wait. I have a funny feeling it won't be long for you now."

Edwin rolled his eyes as he hung up his call.

Newlyweds, he complained to himself. Always

playing matchmaker.

He sighed, glancing quickly around the terminal and blinking as if the fluorescent lighting was a spotlight. He suddenly felt exposed.

Can't stay in one place too long, he thought. They'll recognize me. Even this early in the morning.

He began walking, scanning the signs and ticking them off in his mind as he passed: Wendy's, Auntie Anne's, a news stand.

No, they probably don't even have tea.

Scowling, he paused briefly as he caught the headlines of *Us* magazine prominently displayed on a rack near the door.

"Who is Edwin Sterling's Mystery Woman?"

Not again? Ridiculous.

As he stood glaring at the headline, he caught a glimpse of something interesting out of the corner of his eye. It was a shapely form gliding through the airport, her bright red, Kate Spade rolling luggage spinning along behind her. His eyes swept from the top of her dark head to the click-clacking of her heels as she disappeared around the corner.

Intrigued, Edwin turned to follow her, convincing himself that it was only because he had to go that way anyway, but as he rounded the corner, he bumped against what felt to his tall but less than athletic frame like a boulder that had somehow taken the shape of a man's arm.

"Scuse me," mumbled Edwin. The large man attached to the boulder arm gave him a grim nod and kept going.

For the first time in a long time Edwin felt like he was on the outside looking in. The large man was one of a pair on either side of a much smaller man. All three men wore suits, but the smaller man was the only one who appeared at ease in one.

Wonder who it is. Clearly those are bodyguards.

But Edwin's mind shrugged them off. He scanned the huddled masses for a sign of the dark hair or the bright red suitcase, but she had disappeared into the crowd. He sighed, disappointed, until his eyes focused on what he had started out looking for in the terminal.

Starbucks.

Not a nice London tea room, but it's Dulles airport, after all, he thought. Can't expect too much in Washington, D.C. And it's better than the news stand.

With long strides, he aimed himself for the cubby-hole version of the famous coffee establishment. There was a short line, and he soon found himself at one of the two registers. He ordered his tea, hoping the barista wouldn't recognize him. His luck held.

Too early in the morning for him, too, I guess.

"Hot tea, please," said a low, female voice next to him. He glanced her way. It was the woman with the red suitcase. He pretended not to notice her as he paid for his drink, but he couldn't help but think how unusual it was to find another hot tea drinker on what he knew would be a scorcher of a day.

I thought that was only a British thing.

As the woman waited at the counter for her drink, Edwin bobbed his tea bag up and down in his cup. From his position near the milk canisters, he had a clear vantage point. She was petite, with dark, long hair that waved over her shoulders. He secretly was pleased that she was dressed in a nice pair of slacks instead of jeans or sweatpants. The slovenliness of airplane travelers these days irritated him. He guessed that she was about his age, in her early thirties. Her accent was American, and her skin was clear and fair, but she had high cheekbones and full lips with a slight Mediterranean flair.

Full, beautiful lips.

Suddenly, as if she could sense his gaze, the woman turned and looked directly at Edwin. He attempted to change the schoolboy half-smile into something sexy, but knew by her amused expression that he had utterly failed. She raised one eyebrow and turned back for her tea, but in that one look, Edwin had seen beautiful, intelligent, hazel eyes.

She joined him at the counter to wait for her tea to steep. Edwin struggled to start a conversation. "Hot tea?" was all that came out. He passed a nervous hand through what was left of his hairstyle.

You're an idiot, his brain screamed at him. You can at least act confident.

"Yes," was her short reply.

"In the summer?"

"Yes," she said, eyeing his cup.

"Me, too," he said. "But I'm British, so..."

She smiled, revealing perfect white teeth.

Better do something, stupid. Don't just stand there grinning at her mouth.

He reached for the milk.

She reached for the half and half.

"American," she said by way of explanation, smiling again.

Edwin stuck out his hand. "I'm Edwin," he said.

"Adriana," she replied, taking his hand. "Adriana Allen."

"Adriana from America," he said, wincing as the words left his mouth.

She laughed. Not a mocking laugh, but a happy, contented, truthful laugh. Edwin thought he would do anything and everything to hear that laugh again.

"Where are you headed this fine morning?" he asked, getting his old confidence back.

"Actually, London."

"Really? Which flight?"

"Flight 1161. What about you?"

"Flight 1161! I guess we're fellow travelers."

"I guess so," she replied with another smile. "Well, it was nice to meet you, Edwin," she said, picking up her tea.

Edwin opened his mouth to speak, but she had already wheeled her red suitcase into the crowded terminal again.

He furrowed his brow. He wasn't used to a woman being indifferent to him. He was used to being the one trying to escape the conversation. As much as he told himself it was a nice change, he wasn't sure he liked it.

He decided to head toward the gate, even though common sense told him he should go to the private lounge to wait for the flight. Fewer people and fewer unwanted intrusions of his privacy. But he couldn't get Adriana out of his mind.

Once or twice he got second glances from people passing by. One teenaged girl whispered, "It's Dr. Hanover!" to her friend and pointed him out. Edwin pretended not to notice as she took a stealthy photograph.

At the gate he saw no sign of his mysterious fellow traveller. He seated himself in a corner of the terminal near their gate to wait. Perhaps she went to the lounge? He consulted his watch. Only twenty minutes until boarding. Might as well stay at this point.

Across the aisle Edwin noticed two middle-aged women whispering together and consulting their iPhones as they eyed him curiously.

Googling to see if I'm him.

He wheeled his carry-on bag protectively in front of him.

There was a sudden spurt of giggling and excited movement from the women across the aisle, although when Edwin glanced over, they pretended not to notice.

Yes, you were right. I am Dr. Hanover.

The character of Dr. Hanover had rocketed Edwin into super-stardom. Until that breakthrough show, Edwin had worked hard as an actor, and was slowly achieving recognition in the industry. But *Dr. Hanover's* immediate success had changed Edwin Sterling into a household name. The show was about Christopher Hanover, a handsome and intelligent doctor who solved crimes on the side. He was brave, he was debonair, he was sharp-witted and sharp-tongued. Essentially, he was everything Edwin wished he could be.

Mentally, he summed up the women across the aisle. Not likely to be a problem. Probably content to take a secret photograph or two, but not ask me to take a selfie with them.

He willed himself to relax in the uncomfortable plastic chair.

I do not need an assistant just to take a flight.

2

As the departure time neared, Edwin shifted in his seat. Surely the lovely Adriana should be arriving at the gate soon. A flash of red suitcase caught his eye, and he stood up, hoping she would see him. Their eyes met, and she smiled at him as she approached.

"Hello again," he said, trying to calm his nerves.

"Hello again," she replied.

The plane began to board, beginning with first class. Edwin hesitated; he was in first class, but was she? As Adriana began to move toward the jetway, he followed, relieved. Inside the plane, he made note of her seat. It was on the far right while Edwin's was on the far left. He grabbed the nearest stewardess, who blushed under his blue-eyed gaze. She nodded and approached Adriana, who was about to stow her suitcase in the compartment above her head. Edwin, who had followed the stewardess, intercepted it.

Adriana appeared confused, and slightly embarrassed.

"The stewardess says I can switch seats," said Adriana. "To that side of the plane."

"Yes, if you'd like," Edwin said with a sheepish grin. "I'd love the company. It's a long flight, you know."

She lowered her head for a moment before agreeing and allowing Edwin to transfer her bag to the other side of the plane.

As she settled herself into the seat nearest Edwin, she shook her head.

"How did you manage that?" she asked.

He laughed.

"I used this look," he said, lowering his chin and raising his eyebrows. His piercing blue eyes had a pleading expression. Adriana smiled as she folded her arms across her chest.

"Besides," he continued, "I knew the seat next to me was empty, because I asked specially for it to be. I like my privacy."

"Oh, I see."

He suddenly felt foolish, explaining it like that. Like a spoiled brat who always gets what he wants. He didn't want to tell her who he was. He liked the feeling of anonymity, of being just like everybody else.

He sighed.

"You see, I'm—" he began.

"I know who you are," she interrupted. "You're the actor who plays that doctor on T.V. The one who solves crimes."

"Yeah," he said, sheepishly. "That's me."

"Don't you people usually have bodyguards or handlers or something?" she asked mischievously.

"Usually I have my assistant or my agent. But this was a quick trip. One night in Washington for a gala. My assistant got sick at the last minute. I figured I could handle myself. Speaking of bodyguards—"

Edwin indicated the small man and his two associates who had just boarded the plane.

"I wonder who that is," he murmured, seeing the man's face for the first time. "He looks somewhat familiar."

The small man appeared to be in his forties, with dark hair that was slightly greying at the temples, and a close-cut beard.

"You don't know?" asked Adriana. "That's Ahmet Tastan. He's the CEO of that Turkish oil company."

"Oh! Now I remember. The survivor."

"Yes," agreed Adriana thoughtfully. "He was supposed to be on that plane that crashed in the Balkan Mountains six months ago, but at the last minute he changed his plans."

"And his father and older brother were both killed," Edwin said, his eyes appraising Mr. Tastan as he was settled into his seat on the other side of first class.

"People said it was terrorism, that they were shot down," Adriana whispered.

"What do you think?" he asked. "Everything seems to trace back to terrorism these days."

She shrugged. "Maybe. But it wouldn't be the first time that a son bumped off his father for the throne."

Edwin shuddered.

Adriana began rapidly texting.

"Sorry," she said. "Just texting my friend, Bethany, to let her know we're taking off."

Edwin suddenly had an uneasy feeling in the pit of his stomach. "Maybe we should leave," he whispered to Adriana. "I mean, if terrorists are after him, maybe we shouldn't be on the same plane with that guy."

"I'll protect you," she said with a grin.

3

The mysterious Mr. Tastan seemed content to sleep most of the flight. At first, Edwin had watched every movement the man or his bodyguards made, expecting a terrorist coup at any moment, but when the first hour proved uneventful, he began to relax. Adriana's conversation also soothed and flattered him.

Normally Edwin would have tried to nap on the eight-hour flight, but he didn't want to miss a moment. It had been a long time since he had met anyone, especially a woman, who treated him like he was—well, normal. She seemed to genuinely like him; he even dared to hope she found him attractive.

"So, what brings you to London?" he asked.

"Work," she replied. "I'm a curator for the Middle East division of my museum, and I'm visiting a friend who works at the British Museum. I'm writing a book, and she's letting me do research there."

"You know, I grew up near the Museum," Edwin explained. "Love it. Haven't been in years, though."

"This will be my first trip," Adriana admitted. "Actually, I'm excited that my trip coincides with a new exhibit opening this week. Cuneiform tablets from Istanbul."

"Interesting," Edwin replied, making a mental note to visit the museum in the near future.

For the cuneiform tablets, of course.

"You're different from what I expected," said Adriana, narrowing her eyes and leaning her head back against the seat.

"What did you expect me to be like?" he asked, doing the same.

Dr. Hanover? he wondered.

"I don't know. Arrogant, maybe. Self-absorbed."

"Thank you."

She laughed.

"Well, you're famous. Famous people can sometimes be—"

"Yeah, I know," he agreed. "Think they're better than everyone else. But I haven't been this well-known all my life, you know. Just since *Dr. Hanover*."

"Is that why you're so down-to-earth?"

Edwin considered the question.

Down-to-earth. I like that. Am I down-to-earth?

"I've been around "famous people" all my life," he admitted. "Because of my parents."

She nodded. Edwin's mother, Portia Valentine, was an actress who, in her heyday, had had almost as much of a fan-following as her son now had. Edwin's father, Sir Thomas Sterling, was in the Foreign Office, and was a well-known face in Downing Street.

"I always admired, whether they were in politics or on the stage, the ones who were real in their down time. Who didn't always play a part. My parents were like that, growing up. When they were at home, they were just my parents. Quirky. Annoying sometimes. Not perfect. Just—real."

"That's healthy, don't you think? Mentally?" she asked.

"It takes a lot of effort to play a role," Edwin agreed. "You have to constantly think, because it's not the real you. I couldn't possibly keep it up all the time. It's exhausting."

She frowned, as if thinking deeply about something. Then she shook it off.

"Well, I like the real you," she said.

On the escalator in Heathrow Airport, Adriana checked her phone. "My friend, Bethany, is waiting for me in baggage claim," she said.

"Thank you for keeping me company," said Edwin. "I have been so famished for intelligent conversation."

Adriana smiled up at him. "It was very nice to meet you, Edwin Sterling," she said. "I hope I didn't irritate you too much. I've been told I have strong opinions!"

"No. Actually, you're very—inspiring."

Ask her. Ask her, you fool.

"I'd like to see you again," he blurted out suddenly.

She drew in her breath, looking at him cautiously, as if she were being watched.

He wondered why she hesitated. They had gotten along so well.

She's not in to me. I'm so vain. I just assumed—

"Yes, okay," she said finally. "But I don't have a lot of time. Work comes first."

"Sure, of course," he agreed, relieved.

When they arrived at baggage claim, Adriana's friend was waiting. Bethany Cartwright was an American, but she had lived in London for several years working as a curator for the British Museum. She was slightly plump and wore no make-up, and her blonde, frizzy hair hadn't seen the inside of a salon in months.

As they approached, her blue, spectacled eyes widened and her mouth fell open slightly. Around her, on every side, other people did the same. Some glanced at Edwin furtively, while others gawked in groups, waiting for their chance to approach him for an autograph.

"Bethany, this is—Edwin," said Adriana with a knowing look to her friend. "We met in the Dulles airport."

Bethany recovered herself and stuck out her hand, "Hello, Edwin," she said with a grin. "Nice to meet you!"

"The pleasure is mine," he said.

"So, I'll call you," he said, turning to Adriana.

"You don't need to get your luggage?" she asked.

"No, all I have is this carry-on. One night trip, remember. It's best for me to keep moving, anyway. Loitering causes problems," he said, eyeing the interested onlookers.

"It's good that it's eleven o'clock at night," said Bethany. "I bet you couldn't move in here during daylight hours."

He nodded with a grimace. He leaned over and gave Adriana a kiss on the cheek.

"See you soon," he whispered. He walked briskly toward the exit. Only a few brave fans followed after him for an autograph, but he heard the excited screams of a group of teenaged girls behind him as he passed through the automatic doors.

As Bill, Edwin's driver, loaded his bag in the car, Edwin noticed a large, black limousine parked nearby.

Our Mr. Tastan, I'm assuming.

As if on cue, the man himself walked briskly through the airport doors and headed for the limousine. The two men's eyes met briefly. Edwin got the sense that the older man had sized him up in those few seconds, as if he'd read Edwin's history and weighed his worth. He gave Edwin a nod, as if to say he had passed the test. Edwin nodded back.

As he stepped into the back of his own car, he wondered if passing Mr. Tastan's test was a good thing.

4

"So, what's her name?"

"Whose name?" asked Edwin, turning to his friend, Phillip. They were jogging side by side on treadmills in Phillip's home exercise room.

"Your Mystery Woman. Your secret girlfriend the papers say you have. You keep telling me she doesn't exist, but this time—I don't know. You're different."

"What do you mean?"

How could he possibly know?

"You're extremely quiet, and you're smiling to yourself. You never smile when you run. You hate exercise. You only do it because Dr. Hanover has to be fit."

"I'm smiling right now. See?" declared Edwin, showing his teeth. Phillip wasn't convinced.

Edwin had been friends with Phillip Kingsley-March since they were teenagers and had attended the same boarding school. Phillip was the second son of an Earl, and had been handed a place in his father's bank after he graduated from university.

"So, who's the Mystery Woman?" continued

Phillip, undaunted. Edwin turned off his treadmill and threw him an irritated look as he wiped his forehead with a towel.

Should I tell him? Would she mind?

Phillip stopped, too. "I'm right, aren't I? Did you meet someone in D.C.?"

"Yes, and no," Edwin replied. Phillip waited.

"Okay, I met someone in the airport and we talked on the plane for about eight hours straight. It was the most stimulating conversation I've ever had."

"Thanks," said his friend.

"Not that our conversations aren't stimulating," said Edwin. "But she's just—we talked about everything. Cosmology, theology, anthropology, history. I've never met a woman who had the same interests as me. Not the same opinions, though. Have you ever heard of the Cambrian explosion?"

Phillip shook his head.

"Well, she was completely infuriating. And yet, completely exhilarating."

"What about looks?"

Edwin gave a slight smile. He thought of her smiling eyes and the way she had pulled her hair back from her face as she leaned against the airplane seat beside him.

She's perfect.

"She'll do," he said aloud.

"Are you going to see her again?" asked Phillip.

"I hope so. If she doesn't cancel. We're having dinner tonight. She's here doing research at the British Museum."

"Speaking of the Museum, I have to get a shower. Have to be the face of the bank at some speech or other. Dad's one of the Museum Trustees, but he always manages to get me to go to these things instead. The CEO of Kara Inci is here launching the new exhibit they paid for."

"Kara Inci, the oil company?"

"Yeah. From Turkey."

"That's odd. He was on my plane. Mr. Tastan, right?"

"That's the one. Lots of fuss about him since the plane crash. Bodyguards and everything. Anyway, he's made some kind of an arrangement with the Archaeological Museums in Istanbul. They're loaning us some of their treasures. Lots of cuneiform tablets and stuff. There's even the world's oldest love poem. That should interest you."

"Wait a minute," said Edwin, remembering something. "Did you say cuneiform tablets?"

"Yeah."

"Want some company?" Edwin asked.

His friend eyed him suspiciously.

"You want to go to a museum gallery opening?"

"I've always loved the museum," remarked Edwin, defensively. "And Adriana might be there. She mentioned something about this exhibit."

"Adriana! The name, finally!" said Phillip, triumphantly.

Phillip's wife, Brenda, poked her head in.

"Are you staying for lunch, Edwin?" she asked. "If so, I need to tell Cook."

"No, but thanks. Got to get home so I can change."

"He has a hot date at the Museum," explained Phillip.

Edwin rolled his eyes. "I'll meet you there."

Walking through the ornate gateway to the British Museum brought back memories. It had been years since he had passed through the doors. When you grow up within miles of the place, you can visit often, and Edwin had. He knew the permanent collection well. But lately, his schedule hadn't allowed for much free time, and what free time he had, he spent elsewhere. He was surprised to find that he missed it.

He headed through the Egyptian exhibits until he found the Arched Room, which housed the Department of the Middle East. It was a huge room, built in the early 1800's, with large arched doorways, floor-to-ceiling bookshelves, and wooden drawers filled with countless treasures from antiquity.

A crowd had already gathered. Edwin searched the room for Phillip and found him standing toward the back of the group.

"Where's your Mystery Woman?" he asked immediately.

Edwin shook his head.

"Don't know. I texted her an hour ago, but she never texted back."

He scanned the crowd for her. It was mostly made up of historian-types: professors with shocks of uncombed hair worn long like Einstein because hair appointments took away from their studies, or women wearing long, flowing skirts and birkenstocks. There were also a number of businessmen in suits and ties, like Phillip, sent to represent their company's support of the exhibit. No one seemed to notice Edwin.

Probably not a *Dr. Hanover* crowd.

Mr. Tastan, looking dapper in a three-piece suit, was surrounded by grinning museum directors near a podium at the front.

Edwin nervously took stock of the room, searching for anyone who looked like a terrorist.

What does a terrorist look like, really?

He spotted the two bodyguards easily enough, standing stoically in the front row, but they were the only conspicuous people he noticed.

Someone approached the microphone, tapping it and clearing his throat.

"I'm Dr. Desmond Hall, one of the Trustees of the British Museum. On behalf of the Museum, I'd like to thank you all for coming. We are so grateful for Kara Inci's generous gift that enabled us to make this exhibit possible. The museum of the Ancient Orient at the Archaeological Museums in Istanbul has one of the largest collections of cuneiform tablets in the world, and we are thrilled to have some of those priceless artifacts here under this roof! Mr. Ahmet Tastan, the CEO of Kara Inci, has come all the way from Turkey to be with us here for the opening of the exhibit. Mr. Tastan!"

There was enthusiastic applause as Mr. Tastan made his way to the podium. For the first time, Edwin noticed there was a television crew set up to record the speaker's words for posterity.

Mr. Tastan smiled genially over the crowd, seemingly at his ease, yet Edwin could see a deep melancholy hidden in his dark eyes. The man intrigued Edwin. How difficult it must be to make public appearances after suffering such loss. He caught himself making a mental note for a future role, on the chance that he ever had to portray a man like Mr. Tastan.

"My friends," began Mr. Tastan, "it is my pleasure to represent my nation of Turkey in this act of cultural exchange. Just as the cuneiform tablets represent the beginning of writing in all of human culture, Kara Inci, along with my brothers here in the United Kingdom, wish to unite the world with mutual understanding and appreciation, through history, art, and cultural endeavors, like this exhibit, and with new and improved business alliances that bring nations together instead of dividing them apart. We at Kara Inci—"

A sound like a large breath of air passed over Edwin's head, followed by a quick groan. Out of the corner of his eye, Edwin caught a glimpse of something dark falling to the ground behind him. It landed with a thud that echoed eerily in the quiet room. Edwin's eyes locked with the man at the podium, and in a split-second he watched the melancholy politeness in Mr. Tastan's eyes change to fear. His well-manicured hands were gripping the sides of the podium. The audience waited patiently, wondering why he had stopped his speech.

Edwin turned to look behind him, but a second or two passed before he recognized what it was he saw lying in a crumpled heap on the marble floor.

A man.

Looking up, he saw something attached to a stand, like a camera tripod. But it wasn't a camera.

"It's a gun!" he said aloud, surprised. His voice

ricocheted through the silent room.

Before Edwin's mind had caught up with what his eyes had seen, people around him were screaming and throwing themselves to the ground. He whipped around. Mr. Tastan was completely engulfed by his bodyguards, who were hurriedly assisting him out of a side door. The museum directors, hunched and panicked, followed them out.

"Ed! Get down!"

Phillip yanked on his arm and pulled him to the floor.

"What just happened?" Edwin asked, staring at eye-level at the apparently dead man on the floor at the back of the crowd. Blood slowly oozed in a puddle under his head. Edwin turned away as he realized the man had been shot in the forehead through a dark ski mask he was wearing.

"I don't know. Just stay down until somebody tells us this is over!" whispered Phillip. His usually composed face was tense with fear.

From the ground, Edwin glanced upward to the spot the man had been when he fell. There seemed to be a second level to the Arched Room, a kind of iron balcony, like a catwalk, about twenty feet above their heads.

To reach the second tier of books and drawers, Edwin assumed.

Although the rest of the room was brightly-lit, the upper level was in shadow. He could still see the gun on a tripod, pointed toward the podium at the front of the room.

This was an assassination attempt.

But someone had assassinated the assassin instead.

Security guards surrounded the dead man, and others began ushering people out of the room. Edwin thought he recognized Adriana slipping through an exit. He headed that direction, hoping to catch up, but the crowd was log-jammed at the doors, not letting him pass. Whoever it was had already slipped out of the room.

He turned to look for another exit.

"Edwin Sterling?"

A young woman grabbed his arm as he realized, too late, that the television crew was still filming. His shoulders dropped as he vainly scanned the room for a way of escape.

"I didn't know you would be here," continued the reporter without relinquishing his arm. She was a young woman who probably thought she had been given the rookie assignment of the year, and was only thinly veiling her immense excitement as she turned again to the camera. "Tell us, Edwin. What just happened?"

She thrust a microphone in his face.

"Well, I'm just as in the dark as you," he began politely. "I think someone was trying to kill Mr. Tastan, and he was shot instead." He indicated the gun that was barely visible in the catwalk shadows.

"Shot? But we didn't hear any shots fired!"

"Well, I think it had a silencer," Edwin replied.

"Shocking. Really, a shocking day for everyone. Where were you when it happened?"

"Actually, I was almost right underneath him. I heard what sounded like a breath going over my head, and then the guy fell right behind me."

The reporter gave her most exaggerated look of shock and amazement.

"Do you mean, you could have been killed today?"

"Well, not exactly. I mean, I suppose if the guy had fallen on me, it wouldn't have been the greatest—"

She turned dramatically to the camera.

"Edwin Sterling nearly lost his life today at the British Museum when someone tried to kill Kara Inci CEO Ahmet Tastan."

Brilliant.

5

Several hours later, Edwin was seated at a dimly-lit table in the Bella Luna restaurant, feeling like a man in a dream. He gazed across at his companion.

She's so beautiful.

Adriana's black dress accentuated her fair skin and dark hair, and her eyes were luminous in the candlelit ambiance.

This isn't real, he thought, his mind racing through the crazy events of the day up to then. *And yet, here she is, this beautiful woman, as if I deserve her.*

Say something, say something, stupid. Don't just stare into her eyes like some kind of love-sick puppy.

"I hope you're having a nice time on your trip so far," he said, silently kicking himself.

Brilliant. What a way with words.

"Yes. Except for the excitement today," she replied.

"Of course."

"You were on T.V.," she said.

Edwin cringed.

"Was I? Wrong place, wrong time."

"I'm sorry I missed you today. I had turned my

phone off."

"You know, I thought I saw you, going out one of the exits."

Her eyes flickered for a moment.

"Couldn't have been me," she replied coolly. "I wasn't in that part of the building. I was doing research in another room. I heard the hysteria, though. It was so inconvenient to have to evacuate."

"The news reports say it really was what I thought, an attempted assassination of Mr. Tastan," said Edwin. "But the would-be assassin was shot before he could do his job."

"Yes," she agreed. "Can you believe we were all on the same plane together? I'm glad nothing happened on the flight. But I kind of wish I had been in the room with you. It must have been exciting."

Edwin shook his head. "I'm glad you weren't. It was a dangerous situation."

In his mind's eye he saw the dead eyes of the assassin staring out of his black ski mask.

Adriana raised an eyebrow at him. "I've taken care of myself for a long time now," she said.

"Maybe it's time for someone else to look after you," he replied quietly. She let out a slow sigh, looking away.

You idiot. You embarrassed her. You're moving too fast.

"Will you be sight-seeing at all?" he asked, changing the subject.

"Well, I'll have time for a little. I'd like to visit Kensington Palace."

"You'll love it. Unfortunately, the Duke and Duchess are in Australia, or I could introduce you."

Adriana laughed.

"I'm serious," said Edwin, confused. "Are you going by yourself?"

"Yes. Bethany has to work. But I'll be all right."

"If you'd like company..." suggested Edwin, using his best persuasive look.

She smiled. "Don't you have work to do or something?" she asked.

"I'm between jobs," he admitted. "We'll film more *Dr. Hanover* in the autumn. So, if you need a chaperone—"

"If you're sure you don't mind? I really can handle myself. I'm sure I won't be in any danger, as long as I steer clear of Mr. Tastan," she joked.

"I don't doubt that you can take care of yourself," Edwin replied, "but it would be an honor to accompany you."

Adriana studied him, her chin leaning on her hand.

"What?" he asked, feeling under the microscope.

"I'm just trying to figure you out," she said. "I

googled you."

"Oh, Lord!" he said, rolling his eyes.

"Yes, I did," she laughed. "Because I had a weird thing happen to me in the airport after you left. A teenaged girl came up to me and said, 'You're her, aren't you? The Mystery Woman?' I had no idea what she was talking about, until Bethany told me. She said it's in all the tabloids."

Embarrassing.

"Oh, that. I'm afraid it is. Fun and games for them, I suppose."

"Yet, you never mentioned her to me. You invited me to dinner. And now you're wanting to go with me to a public place, full of tourists. So it makes me wonder, what will your secret girlfriend think of you spending time with some American?"

"Well, she won't think anything of it. She doesn't exist."

"Oh?"

"No. I don't know who started it. All of a sudden one day I had five reporters at my door asking about my "mystery girlfriend". And of course, the more I denied it, the more they assumed it to be true. That I was hiding something, or someone. Since then, anytime I go near a woman, they wonder if it's the 'mystery woman'."

"That sounds extremely inconvenient."

"It is, really. I have to assume it's these online publications trying to get publicity for themselves. It's like they thrive on drama, whether it's true or not. My friend Charles Nettles is a good example. Great actor, loving husband and father. I had dinner with him and his wife one night, and they were completely head over heels for each other, and literally the very next day the headlines read that their marriage was on the rocks."

"So it's a publicity stunt."

"I guess, but not for us. I mean, we get the publicity as well, but not the kind I want. Not what's real. Talk about my acting skills, or lack thereof, or what film I'm working on. That's the kind of publicity I want."

"I've found that people believe what they want to believe," said Adriana thoughtfully. "They want to put people on a pedestal, make them a god or goddess who can do no wrong, and then, when they find out you're human after all, they're the first to drag your face in the mud."

"But why would they want me to have a mystery girlfriend?" he asked.

"Romance," she said with a shrug. "Surely, Dr. Hanover would have a girlfriend!"

He laughed. "I don't have any real damsels in distress to save. That's what you're saying."

"Exactly!" she said. Then she looked thoughtful again. "Why don't you have a girlfriend, Edwin?"

He sighed, leaning back in his chair and drumming his fingers nervously on the tabletop.

Why? he wondered to himself. Why don't I? Because I'm not as cool as Dr. Hanover.

"I've had girlfriends before," he said aloud. "I've had a few flings with actresses I've worked with, but no one who really seemed—compatible. Long-term, you know? Before the show became popular, it wasn't so bad, but since then, it's difficult—almost impossible—to meet anyone naturally. How can I? They either think they know me, based on the characters I play, and they're disappointed when I'm different, or they're—enamored with me. They're a fan."

"They put you on a pedestal."

"Yes! Like a god. Only I'm not a god. Far from it."

"There's only one God," Adriana said.

"And his name's not Edwin!" he agreed. "It's just fantasy again. Not reality. I have trouble finding the real thing. And that's, unfortunately, very important to me."

"Why unfortunately?"

He sighed. "Because it makes for a very lonely Edwin."

Shouldn't have said that. Now she pities me.

Adriana reached across the table and squeezed his hand compassionately.

"Well, I hope," she said, "I hope our—friendship—can ease some of your loneliness."

"I hope so, too," he replied.

As they left the restaurant, Edwin took her hand. It felt small and vulnerable in his, and it made him feel like her protector. He looked down into her upturned face to find her smiling at him.

She looks happy. Really happy. She makes me happy.

Just then, flashes lit up the night.

Photographers, Edwin realized. Paparazzi, outside the doors of the restaurant.

How did they find us? Irritating.

He looked down at Adriana as they rushed toward the car. Her arm was up, warding off the flashes.

She looks frustrated, he thought. *No, afraid.*

"Edwin! What was it like to be in the line of fire today?" shouted a reporter.

"Edwin! Is this your Mystery Woman?"

They jumped into the backseat of the car that was waiting for them.

"I'm so sorry," Edwin apologized.

"I don't know how they find me."

"It's okay," she said, catching her breath as the car

pulled away. "It's part of you." "I'm afraid you may be on the pedestal with me, now."

She shook her head. "They may think we're playing parts in their fantasy," she said, "but we're not actors tonight. Not to each other."

"This is real?" he asked.

"This is real."

He still had her hand in his. He twined her fingers with his and leaned his head back against the seat. He sighed, as if a burden had been lifted.

This is real.

6

The next morning, Edwin's mother called him as he was eating breakfast.

"Darling, I must meet her. You really must bring her over for dinner."

These days, Portia Valentine was semi-retired and spent most of her time worrying about her unmarried, only son.

"Mother! What are you talking about?" Edwin asked.

"Your Mystery Woman, of course. The one whose picture is all over the news. 'Edwin's Mystery Woman photographed outside the Bella Luna restaurant'. She's just lovely, Edwin. You must bring her over."

"Mother, we've just met. That was our first date. I think that would be a bit premature."

"Nonsense," his mother scolded. "I insist."

"Thank you for asking about my near-death experience at the Museum yesterday," he said sarcastically.

"Oh darling," crooned his mother, "they weren't aiming for you."

At least his mother knew the real story when she

saw it.

He hung up, wondering what Adriana would say about her new-found fame. And his mother's insistent invitation. He quickly looked up the story. Sure enough, his and Adriana's faces were all over the internet.

"Mystery Woman Revealed! Dark-haired beauty caught leaving the Bella Luna with Edwin Sterling."

"Edwin Sterling has secret rendezvous with Mystery Woman after near-fatal event at British Museum."

It was matched with several snapshots of the two of them holding hands, looks of surprise on their faces. One lucky photographer had captured them first, gazing into each other's eyes. Edwin quickly saved the photo to his desktop.

He went back to his coffee and eggs and clicked on BBC World News.

"Some are calling the dramatic events at the British Museum yesterday an act of terrorism," said the young female reporter from the day before, standing in front of the museum gates, "but so far, no groups are taking responsibility. The British government has publicly apologized to Mr. Tastan, and the Foreign Secretary has assured his safety for the remainder of his visit. Kara Inci, Turkey's biggest oil company, has seen its share of tragedy in recent months, with the death of former CEO Anwar Tastan and his eldest son, Burak. Both were killed in a plane crash in the Balkan Mountains in Bulgaria last spring. Ahmet Tastan, the second son, was scheduled to have been on the plane that fateful day, but decided to stay behind in Sofia. Although there is no link with any known terrorist groups, many have speculated that the plane was shot down by a militant group unhappy with Kara Inci's recent trade negotiations with the United Kingdom, and with America. The company owes its success to the discovery of large oil deposits in the Kirikkale province, and if the trade negotiations go well, Kara Inci will single-handedly change Turkey from a country that has always imported oil to one that will be exporting it. Consequently, tensions are high in the Middle East, as this puts cracks in the dam that has controlled the flow of oil in the region for decades."

Probably terrorists after all. Out for the last brother.

But who shot the terrorist?

Who is she? Inquiring minds want to know.

It was a text from his assistant, Jen.

A friend, he texted back.

More work for David, she teased.

He winced. David was his publicist. It probably would be more work for David. David was a sharp-dressing ladies' man in his mid-forties, who was just as concerned about his own image as he was about his client's. Edwin had already heard from him and from Debra, his agent, last night after the Museum story had aired.

"What the heck did you think you were doing, almost getting shot like that?" were David's first words to him. "What were you doing there, anyway? Did Debra send you? Some kind of "cultural ambassador" or something? I know I didn't send you there. Lucky for you, the fans are all in an outrage that you were in danger. I can't wait to see what the tabloids will do with this."

Edwin was not so eager.

Debra's response at least showed more motherly concern. She was in her sixties and was a friend of his mother's who tended to coddle him along, as if he were a naive child who needed to be taken care of.

"Edwin, you really must be more careful. That was a close call."

"It wasn't me they were after," he had reminded her.

"Nevertheless. We can't have Dr. Hanover in the hospital. What will the Hanoverians think?"

The Hanoverians were what Edwin's loyal fans called themselves.

After Jen's texts came another call, this time from Phillip.

"The Mystery Woman, at last."

"Don't gloat. You know I hate all this paparazzi stuff," he said, stuffing the last of his toast in his mouth.

"How was your hot date? Other than the paparazzi ending?"

"She was perfect—it was—great. Really great."

"It looks like you were all googly-eyed over her."

Edwin sighed. "It was our first date. I wasn't googly-eyed."

"Pictures don't lie. If I didn't know any better, I'd say you had it bad. Real bad."

"I'm not in love with her, if that's what you think. I've only known her a few days."

"You just said she was perfect."

"I meant great. She's—she's wonderful and great."

There was a long pause.

"I'm not in love with her!" Edwin insisted.

"Okay! I'm not accusing you! But, for what it's worth, she's very pretty."

"Thank you."

"You're welcome. Brenda says bring her over and we'll interrogate her."

"Nothing doing."

"Fine. Well, just be careful. Most things that seem too good to be true, are."

Edwin rolled his eyes. "I appreciate your support."

"Just looking out for you, mate."

Edwin threw his phone down on the sofa. "I'm not in love with her," he declared to the bust of Shakespeare sitting on his bookshelf.

7

As he walked toward Kensington Palace, Edwin suddenly felt exposed. Maybe this was a bad idea. I'll be recognized for certain.

Should've worn the hat.

David had warned him against public appearances.

"Stay low right now," he had urged. "I know you like this girl, but after the Museum thing and the Bella Luna thing, if you don't want the paparazzi following you around, just stay at home or something."

Good advice.

But I can handle myself in public. It's not like I'm in danger.

He saw Adriana standing just inside the Palace Gate, off of Kensington Road. She waved and smiled. She had wanted to meet him there instead of having him pick her up.

She's very independent. American. That's okay.

"Hi," he said as he approached her.

"Hi," she replied. She seemed out of breath, and her cheeks were more pink than usual.

"Did you find the place all right?" he asked. "I

worry about you wandering about the city on your own."

"No problems," she said.

"Well then, why don't we go ahead—" he paused as he saw something out of the corner of his eye. On Kensington Road he saw flashing lights of police vehicles.

"What's going on over there?" he asked.

"Not sure," she said, following his gaze. "Car accident?"

"It doesn't look like it," he said, squinting. "It looks like something's happening in front of that block of flats."

She shrugged. "We could walk over," she suggested.

"No," he said. "It's none of our concern. Let's go on."

They took the Broad Walk to the Palace. The day was warm for June. The sun shining through the branches of the oak trees made dappled pictures on the grass below. Edwin was thankful he could put on his sunglasses to hide his face a little better. He stole a furtive glance at Adriana walking beside him. She seemed to be relaxing as they walked. Why was she tense before? Nervous to see me again?

"Ready to get on the pedestal?" he teased, wondering if that had been her source of concern.

"Bethany didn't want me to meet you today,"

Adriana admitted. "She's concerned that the paparazzi will be out in full force since the other night."

"Well, Bethany could be right," he agreed.

Note to self: get on Bethany's good side. Never good for the best friend to be against you.

"David, my publicist, agrees. He told me to stay low this week."

"Maybe this was a bad idea," she suggested.

He shrugged. "We can't hide away because someone might take a picture. We have lives, too."

She nodded.

"It was kind of weird seeing myself online," she said.

"But you looked beautiful," said Edwin. "My mother agrees."

"Oh dear."

"Yes. I'm afraid so. She saw the paparazzi pictures. Her housekeeper, Millicent, is to blame. She keeps teaching Mother new tricks. I'm not sure I like having her computer-literate. She can be a bit of a troublemaker."

Adriana laughed. "Well, you're blessed to still have her with you. I wish I still had mine."

"I'm so sorry!" said Edwin.

Good show. Bring up the memory of her dead parent.

"It's okay," she said, her eyes on the ground.

"What happened?"

She shook her head as if to ward off any more questions. "I don't want to talk about it. Not right now."

They continued on in silence.

Kensington Palace had been home to several Kings and Queens of England; it was even the childhood home of Queen Victoria. While some royals still lived in flats in the palace, rooms were opened to the public, and the palace, especially the surrounding garden, was a popular attraction.

As they passed a statue of a seated Queen Victoria, Adriana gazed up at her.

"I've always liked her," she confessed.

"Quite a formidable character," agreed Edwin. "She was certainly influential."

Adriana smiled. "A force to be reckoned with, I'm sure," she said, gazing fondly up at the face of the statue. "A woman ruler in an age when women didn't have a voice in politics. Can you imagine the strength she must have had?" she asked, turning to Edwin.

Edwin looked up into the face of the monarch. "She reminds me of my mother," he replied, surprised by that revelation.

"Mine, too," murmured Adriana, turning away.

Inside the Palace, Edwin and Adriana consulted the self-guided tour pamphlet. So far, Edwin had received a few second glances, and caused quite a stir from the young ladies at the ticket counter, but had not caused any major disruptions.

David would be pleased.

Just focus on Adriana. Don't look anyone directly in the eye, and there won't be any disturbances. That works.

So far.

Within the Palace were four staircases with four exhibits. They took the King's staircase first. It was breathtaking, with paintings by 18th-century artist William Kent on the walls and ceilings. In the paintings, life-sized courtiers leaned over banisters and peered down from the ceiling, poised to observe everything and everyone at court.

"It feels like we're being critiqued as we go up," whispered Adriana.

"I wonder if we passed muster and can be admitted into court," Edwin teased.

At the top of the staircase, a group had gathered around an Explainer, who was giving more details about the staircase and the artist who had been commissioned to paint it. As the guide addressed the group, reciting the information like he did each and every day, he gazed lazily across his audience. Suddenly he recognized Edwin and stopped in mid-sentence. The rest of the crowd immediately followed his stare to the back of the group.

"You're Edwin Sterling," he finally managed to say. There was a collective intake of breath.

"All my life," admitted Edwin, matter-of-factly. The rest of the group tittered a bit, staring at him as if he were part of the museum. Only a few noticed Adriana and smiled in her direction.

"Well," continued the guide, clearing his throat. "Welcome to Kensington. As I was saying, the King's staircase..."

His audience immediately turned its attention back to him. Edwin breathed a sigh of relief.

Royalty trumps celebrity, thank God.

He glanced at Adriana. Is she all right? Is she ready to run?

She was smiling up at him.

"Shall we continue, Mr. Sterling?" she teased. He offered her his arm gallantly.

"Yes, Miss Allen. We shall."

The Palace Gardens were extensive and in full bloom, it being summer. Everywhere they looked, there was something new and beautiful. Edwin and Adriana paired off by themselves, although they were not completely out from under the watchful, though

respectful, eyes of the other visitors. Since being recognized by the Explainer, Edwin was finding it difficult to relax; he imagined every bush or thicket as a
potential hiding spot for a journalist or photographer.

Adriana still had a walking tour pamphlet in her
hand and was reading from it as they walked along.

"This is the sunken garden," she said in an offi-
cial-sounding voice. "It was planted in 1908 and
modelled after a similar garden at Hampton Court
Palace."

They passed a family from Germany as they walked
up the Wiggly Walk, a winding path to the sunken
garden; the children giggled and laughed as they ran.

"People, people, people," murmured Edwin,
frowning. Everywhere they had gone inside there had
been people: on the staircases, in the state apartments,
in the grand galleries. Edwin was tired of people.

There's no getting away from them.

And I want her to myself.

He took Adriana's hand and led her to a walkway
covered completely by arched branches of trees.

"Oh, how lovely!" she exclaimed. She consulted her guidebook. "The Cradle Walk surrounds
the sunken garden, with arched viewpoints—" She
looked up as the branches gave way to an archway at
the foot of the sunken garden pool, giving a dazzling
view of the fountains and flowers. Each terraced level

was vibrant with color; deep purple and red pansies, English lavender, and red and pink roses led down to a rectangular pool with a central fountain. She stood enraptured for a moment.

"Don't you think roses are the most beautiful flower in the world?" she asked.

"Yes," Edwin agreed as he impatiently pulled her along, away from the view of others, to a secluded bench under the tunnel of tree branches.

No people. No watchers.

Before sitting down, however, he couldn't help taking a peek through the branches behind them.

No paparazzi.

"The Cradle Walk," continued Adriana from her guidebook, undeterred, "is an arched arbour of red-twigged lime trees."

She gazed above her at the entwined branches.

"Just think, Edwin. These lime trees have been here since 1908!"

Edwin pulled in closer to her, allowing her body to lean against his chest.

"Fascinating," he said into her hair.

She paused for a moment, as if catching her breath.

"The lime trees have been cut back to the ground," she continued reading as he kissed her temple. "To preserve the original tree stock and allow new stems to be trained over the framework of the bower."

She turned toward him. "You're not paying attention," she whispered, smiling.

"Oh, I'm paying very close attention," he whispered back, leaning his forehead against hers.

"To the guidebook?" she asked.

"To you."

Edwin cautiously leaned his face closer to hers. His lips found hers. She returned his kiss, shyly at first, reaching up to touch his cheek with her hand. They kissed again, more boldly now, more passionately.

She pulled back suddenly, shaking her head. "No, Edwin."

"I'm sorry," he apologized.

Too fast. Slow down, you idiot.

"No, don't apologize," said Adriana. "I just—I can't."

She stood up and paced back and forth in front of the bench.

Edwin stiffened. "You're not attracted to me, are you?" he asked, suddenly and pathetically.

Adriana giggled softly, turning to look at him. "Quite the opposite, I'm afraid."

She likes me. Then what's wrong?

"Bethany doesn't like me. Is that it?" he asked, frowning.

"No. It's my fault," Adriana continued. "I mean, yes, Bethany was against it from the start, but, she's my friend, not my mother. I just thought I could handle it. But I can't, obviously."

"Handle what?"

She sighed. She sat down beside him again.

"When we first met, I thought, what's the harm? Talk to him. You'll never see him again. But then you wanted to see me again! I convinced myself that we could be friends, that I wouldn't allow myself to get close to you."

"What's wrong with getting close to me?"

She bowed her head, avoiding the intensity of his gaze. "It's work," she explained without lifting her eyes. "I need to concentrate on work right now."

"Work," he repeated, unconvinced.

She nodded, clenching her jaw. "Yes. I need to give my full concentration. I can't be distracted by— by anything."

"So what does this mean?"

Please don't say it.

"It means that, after today, I can't see you again," she said. "I think that will make it easier for both of us."

She said it.

Edwin's heart sank.

"Because I kissed you?" he asked.

"No," she said, lifting her eyes to his. "Because I kissed you."

Edwin stood up and walked a few steps away. He ran his hands through his hair, as if the action would speed up his thinking.

There must be some way. There has to be.

He whirled around. "What if I promise to be your friend. Only. No romance. No distraction."

"Edwin," she said, shaking her head.

He sat down beside her again.

"Please, Adriana," he said, taking her hand. "I've never met anyone like you. I've never met anyone so real."

"So real?" she repeated with a slight snicker.

"These last few days have been some of the best days of my life."

"Mine, too."

"You said the other night that you hoped our friendship would help my loneliness. Did you mean it?"

"Yes, of course! But we don't even live on the same continent."

"Please don't shut me out completely! If you say you can't be distracted right now, I respect that. I don't understand it, but I respect it. But isn't there room in your schedule for friendship?"

Adriana stared down at his hand tightly holding hers. Then she placed her other hand on top.

"Friendship only?" she asked, her eyebrows raised

challengingly.

"I promise," Edwin answered seriously.

For now.

8

They had tea in the Orangery, the white-pillared colonnade that was once Queen Anne's favorite place to entertain. They were greeted by a thin young man with a carefully trimmed beard and chestnut, shoulder-length curls.

"Oh!" he exclaimed as they approached. "It is an honor to seat you, sir. To think, a young Polish man like myself, to have the honor of seating Edwin Sterling! I watch your show all the time! And oh!" he gasped, seeing Adriana. "Is this *the Mystery Woman?*"

Edwin bit his lip and raised his eyebrows.

Not what I need right now.

The Polish maitre'd took the look as a confirmation. He nodded his head back at Edwin confidentially.

He seated them near the window with great enthusiasm.

"Is this okay?" he asked Edwin. "By the *window?* We wouldn't want any *scenes.* I hope no one bothers you. I will *personally* slap them if they try."

Edwin assured him there would probably be no need for slapping any customers. Adriana giggled as the Polish maitre'd sauntered back to his post by the door.

"He's very enthusiastic about his job!" she commented. She seemed amused by his attentions.

Edwin agreed, trying to keep himself from noticing the way her nose wrinkled as she talked or thinking about kissing her lovely lips again.

Friendship. It's all she'll give. Why? He forced the dark, foreboding thoughts to the back of his mind. Don't think about the possible reasons. Don't think about what—or who.

"Just 50 yards away!" a large, American woman was telling her husband at the next table. "Can you believe it, Harold?"

Apparently, Harold couldn't, as evidenced by his grunt as he stuffed a cake into his mouth. Edwin and Adriana exchanged glances. The woman's voice was loud enough for most of the tables near them to hear.

"Really! It gives me the shivers," continued the woman. "To think we could have been blown up!"

"Nothing blew up, Mildred," Harold reminded her. "They dismantled the bomb before it went off." He stuffed another cake into his mouth.

"Well, it could have blown us up. And on our anniversary trip, too."

Curiosity overtook the Polish maitre'd. He swept over to the Americans' table.

"Excuse me," he interrupted. "Are you talking about the *situation* earlier? We heard it was a *bomb threat!* We just couldn't *believe* it! We're all on edge!"

Adriana smiled. "He seems more excited than anxious," she whispered across the table.

"Yes! It has us on edge, as well!" Mildred declared. "We were passing an apartment building just outside the gates of this Palace, and all of a sudden, we were swarmed by all of these men in black! Police and I don't know what else!"

"At an apartment building?" asked the Polish young man. "Oh, you mean a block of flats."

"Apartment, they said," Mildred replied, "although they tell me that's how the wealthy people do hotels here. Fancy apartments."

"Yes, it's true," commented the young man, knowingly. "Fancy, fancy."

"There was a bomb threat," explained her husband. "But they got it. Before it went off, I mean. When we got there, they were just finishing up. Had everything blocked off still, though."

Edwin looked at Adriana. "I guess that's what all the police were doing earlier," he said.

"We must have just missed it," she agreed.

Odd. Terrorist activity again?

"The police were all over the place," said Mildred. "Wouldn't let us get by for the longest time. We thought we wouldn't be able to come to the Palace at all."

The young man shook his head sympathetically.

"And then we get here, and there's no guards or anything! It's strange. Aren't the British concerned about security here at Kensington? I mean, everywhere else we've been, it's those bear-hat boys."

"Oh!" exclaimed the maitre'd, lowering his voice and looking secretive. "They *have* guards. You just won't see them."

"Really?" asked Harold, intrigued.

"Oh, yes," the maitre'd continued. "*Plain clothes.* Walking around the garden among us. You'd never know they were there. Unless you committed a crime, of course." He laughed at his own joke. The Americans laughed with him.

"Well, I'm glad to hear it. It makes me feel a *little bit* safer," said Mildred. "But it really was so awful!" she complained, fanning herself. "I mean, we could have been killed! Blown to bits!"

Harold shrugged his shoulders again and reached for another cake. "It didn't go off, Mildred," he said with his mouth full.

After their meal, Adriana went to visit the ladies' room. Edwin waited outside on the terrace in the clear sunshine. It was a beautiful day, uncharacteristically warm for London in June. He fiddled with his collar and wished he hadn't worn a long-sleeved shirt.

He could see squirrels skittering around under the nearby tall holly trees shaped into hedges that lined the walkway. As he watched one of them scurry under a bush, he noticed a young woman standing behind one of the thickly-leaved hedges.

Paparazzi? No, too timid.

The young woman met his gaze and gathered the courage to come out from her hiding place and approach him.

Fan. She's a fan. Glazed look in her eye.

Pedestal time.

The woman grabbed Edwin's hand and wouldn't let go.

"Oh my gosh. It's really you," she said, blinking.

"Good afternoon," Edwin said politely, glancing quickly around to locate the maitre'd standing in the open doorway behind him.

If I need him.

"I saw you go in the gates, off the street," said the woman, still holding his hand. "I couldn't go into the Palace because, of course, it's a lot of money, but I saw you go in the gates, so I thought, 'I'll just wait for him until he comes out.' Because the garden's free, you know, and I can stand in the garden and wait for you. So I did."

"Well, that's—nice," said Edwin. He tried to pull his hand away, but she held it tightly. He noticed that despite the somewhat erratic look in her eye, the woman was not unattractive.

How does this happen? he wondered. This obsession? Doesn't she know any nice young men?

"Saw you walking with that—girl." Her lip curled slightly at the word. "Tea at the Orangery? That's nice," she continued. "I've had tea here, once, on my birthday. It's nice." She nodded her head up and down, gazing into his eyes, still smiling and looking at him adoringly.

How can this end?

Suddenly, Adriana was at his elbow. Edwin felt relieved. She smiled respectfully at the young woman, although he could tell she knew this was not one of his friends. He watched in surprise as the expression on the young fan's face changed rapidly to one of malicious anger.

"You're the Mystery Woman!" she hissed, letting go of his hand.

Finally. He shook it to help the circulation get started again.

"I saw your picture online!" she growled, stepping closer to Adriana. "You're even uglier in person."

Adriana stared at the young woman with a puzzled expression.

Help, thought Edwin. I'm going to need some assistance here.

"You can't have him, you know," the young woman continued, her hand slipping into her pocket. "Edwin is destined to love me, not you!"

"I don't even know you!" Edwin reminded her, shaking his head.

"But you *will* love me, once you know me!" she said, her attention momentarily on him again. "You're the only one for me, Edwin! And I won't let some mystery woman take away my chance!"

Edwin made silent signs to the Polish maitre'd that help was needed. When he turned back again, he was shocked to see Adriana gripping the fan's arm in midair, a small, switchblade knife glinting in the afternoon sun.

No! Oh, God, no!

Before he could move, it was over. While gripping the young woman's arm, Adriana had stepped toward her, putting her foot behind the woman's legs. She tripped her, and while holding onto her back and still gripping her knife-wielding arm, she gently lowered the woman to the ground. With a flick of her wrist, she then disarmed the woman of the knife, kicked it away, and put her foot against the side of the woman's neck to keep her from getting up.

The young fan began wailing like a child.

"Help! She's trying to kill me! Edwin! Edwin!" she screamed from the ground.

"Oh my gosh! Oh my gosh! Security!" shrieked the Polish maitre'd, rushing toward them. Then he just as quickly rushed back into the restaurant, shouting directions to his startled staff. Seemingly out of nowhere, a man wearing a jogging suit appeared, flashing a security badge. He took over, allowing Adriana to step back.

Edwin stared at her as she looked his way. She seemed embarrassed.

What just happened? How did she know how to do that?

A few of the other tourists noticed the scuffle and stood gaping nearby. It had happened so quickly, there wasn't time for real panic. The aggressive fan shouted insults as she was being dragged off by the undercover guard, who had been joined by two other men from other parts of the garden: one was wearing a business suit and another was in a hoodie.

"Harold, I wonder if that's the bomber?" asked Mildred in a loud whisper from the terrace. Harold shrugged, fascinated by the scene in front of him.

"I guess the maitre'd was right," said Adriana, giggling nervously as her eyes followed the retreating group. "Plain clothes guards."

She's in shock, I think.

I am, too, I think.

Edwin took her in his arms and held her close to him. She allowed it. He could feel her shivering.

My fault. All because of me.

"Adriana, I'm so, so sorry!" he said. "It's my fault. This wouldn't have happened if—if anything had happened to you, I would never forgive myself!" He held her tightly, pressing his lips against her hair. He noticed that he was shivering as well.

They had to wait for the constable to come. He asked a lot of questions, particularly of Adriana. Did they know the perpetrator? What had she said? Why did she want to kill Adriana? It all sounded so preposterous, so like a movie or an episode of *Dr. Hanover*. The Polish maitre'd was only too delighted to give evidence. Edwin hoped his story wouldn't be embellished. But really, it's so absurd already, what difference would embellishment make?

They took a cab back to Bethany's home. Adriana gazed out the window as they drove. Edwin looked over at her. She seemed tense.

I would be, too, if someone had just tried to kill me.

"Where did you learn to do that?" he asked, breaking the silence. "To flip an armed woman onto her back and take her knife?"

Adriana turned toward him.

"Well, she wasn't exactly Chuck Norris," she joked.

"But really, where did you learn that?" he insisted.

She shrugged. "I used to watch my brother's karate classes. I guess I picked up a few things."

"Hmm," Edwin grunted.

Adriana smiled. "The constable didn't believe me, either. But it's true," she said with a shrug. "He asked me who I was working for."

"Like some agency or something?"

"I guess. He wasn't happy when I told him I was a mere historian."

Edwin could hear the constable's sardonic voice in his head.

"Mr. Sterling, what do you know about this Adriana Allen?" he had asked Edwin, privately. "She says she learned to do that by watching her brother's karate classes, but any normal woman would have stepped away from the crazy woman, not toward her. That seems like training, to me."

Any normal woman would have been killed.

9

"It's no longer an invitation, Edwin," his mother said when she called the next morning. "It's a command. I must meet her. Your father agrees. In fact, he's become quite enthusiastic about it."

"Mother—"

"Millicent showed it to me on the—internet—this morning." Edwin's mother still said 'internet' as if it were a foreign name. "'Mystery Woman Saves Edwin Sterling's Life at Kensington!' it says. 'Mystery Woman Revealed—Karate Champ Saves Edwin Sterling From Knife-Wielding Fan!' I must meet the woman who saved my son's life."

"Mother, she didn't save my life. She saved her own life. The knife-wielding fan was after her, not me."

"Nevertheless. She would have saved your life, if you had been in danger. You must bring her to dinner. I will not take no for an answer."

"I'll see what I can do," he said with a roll of his eyes.

He had no idea what Adriana's answer would be to the invitation. When they had arrived at Bethany's home the night before, she was waiting for them. She had seen the fan debacle on the news, and she was not happy. Edwin felt her glowering looks pierce through him as Adriana tried to soothe her friend with explanations. Bethany remained cold toward Edwin and seemed annoyed even at her friend. *I told you so* was written all over her face.

He shook his head. So far, every time he went near Adriana, it ended up in the news. Would she risk dinner with his parents?

While he was in the shower, he had two voice messages from David.

"You are unbelievable!" he said. "I thought I told you to stay at home! Do you realize this is the second close call you've had in less than a week? Twitter is going crazy. But this definitely works in your favor. Sympathetic fans appalled at the crazy one."

A few minutes later he had left another message. "By the way, I am glad you're all right. And I'm glad your "mystery woman" is okay, too. Where did you get this girl? She's great! But stay at home. We've got an interview for two mags next week. I can't have you killed or anything. I want you talking about the new season of *Dr. Hanover*."

As Edwin left his house to join Phillip for lunch,

he was greeted by reporters at his door, asking if this was the mystery woman he had been hiding for so long.

He answered the reporters cleverly, he thought.

"She definitely is mysterious," he said, pushing through the crowd. "Any woman who can disarm a crazy fan in three seconds flat is a woman of mystery."

Not a lie. Not a confession.

But as he walked along, he realized it was true. Adriana was a mystery to him. A museum curator who is a martial arts expert? A historian so engrossed in her work that she doesn't have time for a romantic relationship? Or is there more? Edwin frowned. He wondered what Phillip would say about it.

"It's got to be another man," said Phillip between bites of fish and chips.

"So you don't believe it's work, like she said?" asked Edwin.

"Half the women of the world are dying to go out with you, and the one woman you give that honor to says she just wants to be friends? Come on, Ed. You've got to face the facts. She's the one with the secret relationship."

Edwin pondered the possibility. Her hesitation in the airport when he asked to see her again. The flicker of fear in her eyes when the paparazzi photographed them. Yes, it definitely was fear. Not just annoyance or surprise. Maybe she didn't want someone to see them together.

"But why would she go out with me at all, then?" he asked, half to himself.

Phillip shrugged. "Why do women do anything? I never understand half of what they do."

Edwin frowned, his brow creased with deep lines. He rubbed his hand across his forehead, forcibly smoothing it.

Stress. Got to get some sleep or something.

"It's just like Mary Alice Rowan," said Phillip.

Edwin glared at his friend.

"I can't believe you just brought her up."

Mary Alice Rowan. I never want to hear that name again.

Phillip stopped stuffing his face and contemplated his friend.

"She strung you along so she could meet that guy—what's his name? He was in the theatre with you at school."

"Stephen Quinn."

"That's it. The guy with all the muscles who looked like a GQ model."

Edwin rolled his eyes. "Just because Mary Alice Rowan dumped me for Mr. GQ does not mean it's the same. Adriana's different. She said it was work."

"Let's just be friends, Edwin," Phillip said in his best Mary Alice voice. "I don't like you *that* way, Edwin."

"Shut up."

"I don't want to see you crying yourself to sleep every night again."

"I did not cry myself to sleep!" Edwin insisted, turning red.

Irritating.

Phillip shrugged and attempted to change the subject.

"So, what's happening with the crazy fan?" asked Phillip. "That was something. Never a dull moment with you."

"She's in prison awaiting trial, although she'll probably get away with mental incompetence."

"Do you think Adriana knew her?"

"No," he answered curtly. "Why should she?"

"I don't know. Why should she know how to knock her to the ground and take her weapon? The whole thing is like some kind of *Dr. Hanover* episode. Are you sure no one is following you around with cameras?"

Edwin rolled his eyes. "I've had crazy fans before. What about that woman I caught digging through my garbage? Or the one who kept sending me stuffed animals?"

"Hardly worthy of comparison. A restraining order at best. This is attempted murder, Edwin."

"I know."

Of course, I know. And I don't want to think about it.

"You know, they say that for every ten fans, one of them is a potential threat. All it takes is one little snub," continued Phillip.

"Who says that?"

"I don't know. People."

Edwin considered it. One in ten, a potential threat.

How many fans do I have?

"Are you going to try to see her again?" Phillip asked dubiously.

"The crazy fan?"

"No, Adriana."

"You don't think I should?"

"You're a big boy. You can make your own decisions. But—"

"But you don't think I should see her again."

Phillip spread his hands out. "She's hiding something. That's all I'm saying. Nobody was trying to kill you before she came along."

"Nobody's trying to kill me!" Edwin said.

Too loud. People looking.

"Nobody's trying to kill me," he repeated, more

quietly this time. "She attacked Adriana, not me."

"Mm-hmm."

"Why is this hard to understand? If she'd attacked me, I probably would be dead, because I didn't watch my brother's karate class. I don't even have a brother."

"Mm-hmm."

"Mother wants her to come to dinner."

Phillip brightened. "I think that's an excellent idea."

"You do?"

"Yes. If anyone can interrogate a witness, it's your mother. She'll get to the bottom of your mystery woman before the dessert course."

10

"Now, Mother, she is not my girlfriend," reminded Edwin.

They were seated in the elegant sitting room of his parents' Victorian flat. Edwin had always loved the carved mahogany woodwork and original fireplaces. The sitting room was wallpapered in a rose pattern, and his grandmother's antique furniture was upholstered in chintz. It was a welcoming room.

Adriana had agreed to come to dinner, after careful persuasion by Edwin that it was his mother's invitation to honor her act of bravery, not his.

"I don't understand this 'friendship' request of hers," complained Portia Valentine, her blue eyes flashing. "Why wouldn't she jump at the chance of being with you? Does she have a boyfriend she's hiding?"

Edwin sighed. "I don't know. I hope not."

I really hope not.

"We wouldn't want another Mary Alice Rowan incident," she continued.

"Oh, God," Edwin murmured under his breath.

"When I met your mother, she was engaged to another man," commented his father, his steely-gray eyes twinkling. "I didn't let that stop me."

"I remember," said Edwin. He had heard the story before. Many times.

Edwin's father, Sir Thomas Sterling, was known for his even temper and well-mannered composure in politics. His relationship with Portia Valentine, the famous actress, however, had broken every rule he had set for himself, and tongues had wagged at the time of his romance and marriage. But the test of time had proven that this was no fly-by-night relationship, and Sir Thomas had never regretted his decision.

"It's true, Edwin," his mother agreed. "I was engaged to John Greeves."

"*Sir* John Greeves?" Edwin asked, gaping. This was a part of the story he didn't know.

"Yes," she said, surprised. "Well, of course, he wasn't Sir John, then. He wasn't knighted until he did that Vietnam film everyone was so crazy about. Back then, he was just Johnny Greeves."

"Lord, Mother! I think you could have told me this before! That explains why he avoids me in public."

She waved a heavily-ringed hand at him. "I didn't think it was important. The important part is that

I was engaged, and then your father saw me at the National Theatre. I was playing Nora in *A Doll's House.* He came backstage to meet me, and—"

"And I fell completely in love with you on the spot," added his father, gazing into her eyes.

"He kept asking me to go out with him. Sending me flowers! I kept telling him, 'I'm engaged!' but he wouldn't take no for an answer." She smiled at her husband. "So, I did the only thing I could do."

"And what was that?" asked Edwin.

"I went out with him, of course!"

Adriana arrived punctually. She seemed a little nervous as she was greeted by Edwin's family. Edwin's mother was genuinely pleased with her. She complimented Adriana until the younger woman blushed, thanking her profusely for 'saving her son's life'. Adriana protested, but seemed honored by the attention.

Dinner was excellently prepared, and the conversation went smoothly, despite Edwin's fears. He found himself strangely proud of Adriana's good impression on his parents. He began wondering what the future might hold. Sure, she lives on another continent, but couldn't this somehow work?

If Phillip's right, if there is another man, I could follow in my father's footsteps. Sweep her off her feet.

And into my arms.

Sitting across the table from her, he couldn't keep his eyes off her face as she told a story, with images of himself as the hero running through his brain.

"Edwin!" Portia Valentine's voice broke through his dreams. "I was asking you a question."

"Sorry, Mother. I didn't hear you."

His mother smirked. "Your attention was elsewhere, I see," she said. Edwin could feel his face burning as he tried to recover his composure.

Stay in the moment, Edwin.

"I was asking if you would like to move to the sitting room for dessert, or if you'd rather have it here?"

"The sitting room is fine, Mother," Edwin replied, glad to have some excuse to move out of the awkward situation.

In the sitting room, Sir Thomas managed to secure a place near Adriana.

"So, my dear," he began, "Edwin tells me you learned to defend yourself by watching your brother's karate classes."

"Yes, sir. It's true," Adriana confessed.

"Interesting," Sir Thomas continued, his eyes twinkling beneath tufted brows. "I know a little martial arts, myself."

"Do you?" asked Adriana.

"Do you?" asked Edwin. His father had always

seemed above sweating. He didn't even own a pair of sweatpants.

Sir Thomas nodded. "Learned it in the service. Been a long time now, though. But there are things you never forget. You remember training, once you've had it. You recognize it when you see it. Had mine in Turkey, of all places."

"Turkey? Really?" Adriana replied.

Edwin looked at her. She was smiling, but there was a hint of something in her face—not fear. Maybe caution?

He looked back at his father. He seemed the same, the perfect English gentleman. But there was a tangible tension in the air that hadn't been there before.

"A number of years ago, it's been now," Sir Thomas said contemplatively. "When I was the ambassador."

His eyes glazed over as he drifted back to another time and place.

"Oh, yes," Edwin's mother chimed in. "That was before he met me. Went all over the place in those days. I always tease him that he was a spy!"

Sir Thomas chuckled. "Beautiful country, Turkey," he continued, snapping back into the present. "But a turbulent history. Even in the last century, with the exile of the Sultan and his family and the beginning of the Republic."

He eyed Adriana from under his eyebrows.

"I went back several times to Ankara, in the '80's," he continued. "Just after the coup. Rather a dangerous time. Unpredictable."

"I would imagine so," Adriana said quietly, her eyes on the coffee table in front of her.

"Is that when the Sultan was exiled?" asked Edwin. "Was that the coup?"

"No," Adriana explained. "The Republic was formed after World War I, but there were several coups in the latter half of the twentieth century." She smiled. "Democracy isn't always easy to maintain."

"Lots of interesting things to see and do in Turkey," Sir Thomas continued, as if she hadn't spoken. "Have you been there?"

Adriana shook her head. "Not yet."

"Troy, now that's something to see. It's in the Canakkale Province. Nobody believed it was an actual place, until the 1800's. Thought Homer made it up. But there it was. Just under the surface."

"Have you been there, Father?" asked Edwin.

"Once. It's a place full of mystery," he said, looking at Adriana. "Danger and mystery."

"Oh, my!" Edwin's mother cried. "Mystery! It sounds exciting. You must take me sometime, Thomas."

Sir Thomas chuckled again, losing the serious tone he had been using. "Maybe sometime I will. But not just yet, I think."

"Why would it be dangerous?" asked Edwin. "Isn't it just an historic site?"

"Wars were fought there," explained his father. "Wars are fought there. There's always danger in war, no matter which side you're on. Wouldn't you agree, Adriana?"

"It's part of the risk," she said. Her eyes were bright, and her face was strangely serious.

Odd. Decidedly odd conversation on both sides. Edwin puzzled over the change in his father in particular. He was never known to be boisterous and frivolous like his mother, but he was rarely vague. Is it Adriana? Is he trying to impress her with his mysterious, romantic past?

I suppose even an old man can be silly over beauty.

At the end of the evening, Edwin saw his mother hug Adriana and whisper something in her ear. She blushed, glancing furtively at Edwin. After she left, Edwin cornered his mother.

"What did you say to Adriana?" he asked.

"Oh, I just said that I adored her," she replied simply, waving him off.

"Mother!"

"Well, I do," she protested. "And then I said that she makes my son very, very happy."

Edwin groaned, burying his face in his hands.

11

Edwin and his assistant, Jen, sat across the table from each other in his dining room that doubled as an office.

"Okay, so tell me all about her," Jen demanded, her freckled nose wrinkling as she grinned girlishly at him.

"Don't we have a lot of work to do today?" he stalled. "I thought we had to plan for that interview for *Everyman Magazine.*"

She pretended not to hear.

"According to the internet, you've gone to dinner with her at the Bella Luna, and a mad fan almost killed her in Kensington Gardens. Were you scared, Ed?"

"Me heart was in me crossways!" he said with a perfect Irish accent.

She made a face at him.

Edwin loved to tease his Irish assistant. She was the daughter of a friend of his parents, and Edwin had known her since she was a girl. It irritated him slightly that she had married before him.

"Oh, I meant to ask you," she said, suddenly changing the subject, "Were you there when they had that bomb scare? I wonder if the two things are related?"

"What two things?"

"The bomb and the loony fan. I mean, two weird things on the same day in the same location—"

"It wasn't the same location. They were blocks away," Edwin reminded her.

"Well, close, anyway. Do you think the loony fan sent a bomb to that oil guy?"

Something in what she said made Edwin uneasy.

"What oil guy are you referring to?" he asked, but he knew the answer before she spoke it.

"Mr. Tastin? Tartar? Something like that. The one who was in the news."

"Mr. Tastan?"

"I guess. The one who was almost killed in front of you."

"It was Mr. Tastan who was almost bombed in Kensington?" Edwin asked, his voice strained.

I can't seem to get away from this guy.

"Yes. Where have you been? It's all over the news. Anyway, what if your loony fan planted a bomb, hoping you would walk by and be blown up!"

"You are far too gleeful about it for my comfort," he commented. "And anyway, my 'loony fan' wasn't after my death. She was after Adriana's."

"So, what's she like? You like her, obviously."

"I like her. My parents like her. What's there not to like?" he asked gloomily.

"She's met your parents?" cried Jen. "I didn't realize how serious this was already."

Edwin rolled his eyes. "Back to business, or you're fired," he teased.

Jen obeyed, pulling up his calendar on her iPad.

"Gerald didn't meet my parents until we'd been dating six months," she murmured without looking up.

"She's just a friend," he explained, not very convincingly.

She eyed him with narrowed, green, cat-like eyes.

"Just a friend," she repeated. "Just a going out to dinner friend, meeting your parents friend, saving your life friend. Freaking David out with all the Mystery Woman publicity. That kind of just friends?"

"Yeah," he agreed. "I know."

"I guess you know what you're doing."

Jen went back to her calendar.

Of course I know what I'm doing. Don't I?

Edwin's mind began to wander as she started reading off his schedule for the next week.

The bomb attempt was for Mr. Tastan? Another terrorist act against him. Someone really wants him dead.

The next morning was his *Everyman Magazine* interview. David had made it clear to the interviewer that there would be no mention of Mr. Sterling's personal life. Strictly business. Edwin was looking forward to it. He usually excelled in interviews.

Probably because I like to talk.

Everything had gone well until the interviewer asked him an unexpected question.

"Life's been a bit exciting for you lately," the interviewer had said. "You were there at the British Museum when Ahmet Tastan was nearly assassinated, and then you were in Kensington being attacked by a loony fan at the same time that Mr. Tastan had a bomb threat in his flat!"

"Yes," Edwin had agreed, trying to downplay it. "Pretty scary stuff."

Don't ask about Adriana.

"So, do you think someone is after you?"

"What?"

"Do you think those assassination attempts were really meant for you? I mean, it is odd that you were in the same places at the same time."

"I wasn't really—I mean, no. No, I don't think—"

It had thrown him. His usual cool demeanor was gone.

"You're going to have to scratch that," he had said to the interviewer. "No questions about my personal life."

"It's public information. It's on the news," the reporter had insisted.

"Remove it!"

Later in the day he had a voicemail from David.

"Hey man. Great interview with *Everyman*. By the way, they did agree to take out that part about your life being in danger. No personal questions. I don't know what got into that reporter! But it's interviews like this that really keep you in the public eye. Keep people talking about you, wanting to know what you have to say. And don't let Debra finagle you into doing some stupid alien film or something. Gotta keep the focus on your serious acting skills. I'm in your corner, Ed. You can count on me."

He also had an email from Debra.

"I know David got you those interviews for the magazines. I hope it went well today. But I need you to keep in mind that it's your work that keeps you fresh in people's minds. If David's not careful, he'll have you doing nothing but interviews, and all my hard work getting you leading roles will be for nothing because you won't have time to do them. Have you looked at the script I sent you? It's a Warner Bros. film. They aren't going to wait forever for an answer. Toodles."

Edwin sighed. David and Debra had a constant

love/hate relationship. In public, they smiled and only gave the occasional jab at each other, but behind each other's backs, they waged a war for Edwin's attention and loyalty. Each one wanted to be the more trusted, the more relied on, the more wanted. And both assumed Edwin was oblivious to the power play. It only added stress to his already stressful life.

Don't they know I need them both?

Especially now.

The interviewer had really thrown him. Edwin had never even considered that someone was after him. He found it ridiculous, almost narcissistic, to think that anyone would attempt to kill him. But he had to admit, these were strange coincidences. Bombs, covert assassins, fans with knives. He did seem to be attracting danger lately.

His thoughts turned to Adriana, and he found himself desperately wanting to see her.

It was an hour before closing time when he arrived at the museum. He hoped she would be there. He had taken a risk and not called ahead.

He headed toward the cuneiform exhibit, realizing as he did so that it was a perfectly legitimate excuse for being there. He hadn't had the opportunity of seeing the exhibit, since the last time he was there the museum had been evacuated.

As he entered the gallery he wasn't disappointed.

There she stood, admiring a cuneiform tablet with a regal air. He approached her and stood just behind her, gazing up at the tablet

"Isn't it beautiful, Edwin?" asked Adriana.

Edwin wondered if she had a sixth sense. She hadn't even turned as he approached.

He squinted up at the tablet, brown and un-adorned. Beautiful is not how he would have described it.

A plaque to the side translated the tablet. It was the tablet considered to be the world's oldest love poem. The poem had been written in the 8th century BC by a Sumerian priestess as she was married to the king of Babylon. Edwin read the translation.

> *"Bridegroom, dear to my heart,*
> *Goodly is your beauty, honeysweet,*
> *Lion, dear to my heart,*
> *Goodly is your beauty, honeysweet."*

"It reminds me of the Song of Songs in the Bible," he said, struck by the descriptive language.

She nodded. "How wonderful to be so unafraid," said Adriana.

Edwin wrinkled his brow. "What do you mean?"

She sighed. "Unafraid to express yourself, to pour out your feelings. This writer isn't worried about what her lover thinks of her, or what the world thinks of them. She just comes right out and says what she feels. It's beautiful in its honesty."

Edwin unobtrusively studied her profile. Would she ever feel brave enough to write a love song like that? And if she did, would it be to him?

He shook off the dream he was beginning to spin in his mind. Adriana turned.

"What brought you here?" she asked, pulling her attention away from the tablet at last. "I was going to call you..."

Edwin shrugged. "I've had a strange day. Thought I'd come see the exhibit I never got to see."

She nodded, accepting his excuse. They walked slowly through the gallery while Adriana pointed out her favorites. Edwin was mesmerized by her knowledge, but mostly by the beauty that lit her face when she spoke. Afterward they went up the circular staircase in the Great Court for tea.

To Edwin, the Great Court restaurant always felt like Mount Olympus, with its open-air feel so far above the main floor, and so close to the ceiling of glass skylights above. He squinted at the sky. Gray clouds skidded across it, wraith-like and misty. He imagined the clouds that enveloped Mount Olympus would have also been mysterious and gray like that. Hiding greatness from those below. And the humble from the great.

Tea had just arrived when Edwin noticed the elevator doors open and Bethany enter the restaurant. She hesitated, but came to the table with what Edwin guessed was her attempt at a cordial smile.

"I didn't realize you were here, Edwin," she said, looking quizzically at Adriana.

"He came to see the cuneiform exhibit," she explained quickly to her friend.

"Ah," nodded Bethany, eyeing him like a teacher whose student has just told her the dog ate his homework.

Edwin smiled, but his heart wilted under her gaze.

"I suppose you came to say goodbye."

"Goodbye?" Edwin asked, looking across at Adriana.

There were crimson spots in each of her cheeks and she twisted her napkin in her hands.

"That's what I was going to call you about," she said, attempting a smile. "I leave tomorrow."

"But I thought we had a few more days?" demanded Edwin.

"I did, too. But some things changed, and apparently I'm needed back at home. So—"

Behind her, a group of men entered the dining room from the circular staircase. To Edwin's surprise, he recognized Mr. Tastan and his matching bodyguards. The Turkish gentleman didn't seem to notice them, or anyone else in the room.

Bethany turned away from the elevators.

"The time, Adriana," she reminded her.

Adriana's sharp exclamation brought Edwin's attention back to their table.

"Oh, Edwin!" she said, looking quickly at her watch, "I completely forgot about my meeting with one of the curators! I'm afraid I must be going. Call me later. Please?"

"Yes, of course," said Edwin, still dazed by the news of her departure. He stood as Adriana rose. As he leaned forward to give her a kiss on the cheek, he nearly bumped into Bethany, who seemed to be hovering closer than he realized.

She still doesn't like me.

Adriana and Bethany disappeared down the staircase, leaving Edwin alone with his tea.

I must see her again, he thought. Tonight.

12

Tea by yourself can be an extremely lonely meal. Edwin drained his cup and stood to leave, throwing money on the table to cover the bill. As he crossed the room, his eyes met the gaze of Mr. Tastan. There was instant recognition, and the Turkish man waved him over. He stood and shook hands with Edwin.

"You were at the Exhibition opening," he said in a deep, slightly accented voice.

"Yes. Edwin Sterling."

"Please have a seat. Join us. You are an actor, I am told."

Edwin sat opposite the businessman, struck again by his intense, yet melancholy, deep-set eyes.

"Yes," he replied.

"You like history, Mr. Sterling?"

"Yes," agreed Edwin. "And historians." His eyes strayed to the staircase where Adriana had disappeared.

Mr. Tastan chuckled. "Love. It *is* our written history, is it not?"

Edwin smiled.

"Thank you for arranging the cuneiform exhibit," he said to Mr. Tastan, meaning it. "It's quite a collection."

The other man bowed slightly and lifted empty hands.

"It is important, this. To promote a cultural exchange, goodwill among nations." His eyes darkened as he spoke. He looked intently at Edwin.

"I am raising my brother's children, Mr. Sterling," he said, his mouth grim. "All because someone felt that our company should not expand, should not do business, man to man, with the western world." He leaned forward across the table. "But I will continue the legacy of my father, my brother. I will not let fear keep me from fighting for what is right!"

"So you believe it wasn't an accident? The plane crash?"

Mr. Tastan shook his head. "We were in Sofia establishing trade connections for our company. Sofia, in Bulgaria, is a central route to the West, an important place to have a base of operations. As we prepared to leave, my father asked me to stay in Sofia. He felt something was not quite right, that the deal was more fragile than it appeared."

He paused, eyes on the table. He swallowed visibly and passed a shaking hand across his forehead. "As you know, he was quite right. Had all of us been on that plane, it would have been the end of Kara

Inci. So I must continue, Mr. Sterling. I must finish what my father began."

What a strange day, Edwin thought as he watched Mr. Tastan across the table. God, to have his courage! Here is a wanted man, whose life has been threatened three times, two of those in the last few weeks, and yet he seems more alive, more real, than I could ever be.

He inwardly laughed at himself for allowing the interviewer of *Everyman* to make him think his own life was in danger.

Why would anyone kill me?

13

Edwin waited, seated on a bench in the shadows. He had convinced Adriana to meet him one last time in Kensington Gardens. In their spot, their special place under the lime trees.

He had hoped for a few more days with her, a few more days to figure it all out. But their time was cut short. By what? Or who?

He brushed that thought out of his mind.

He wasn't sure what he was going to say. A monologue about friendship leading to something more? No, she doesn't want something more. Not right now.

He waited there, restless. Will she come? It's getting late.

He consulted his phone. Although it was already nine o'clock, London's summer sun was only just beginning to head toward twilight. Most of the park's visitors had long since gone home to their dinners or back to their hotel rooms. He was alone.

He heard a footstep at the far end of the canopied walk, and he looked up suddenly, eagerly. For a brief moment, he felt a flicker of fear, as if it arrived with the scent of roses on the summer breeze, and just as suddenly faded away.

She stepped into the arbor. The fading sunlight framed her figure as she walked toward him.

She's so lovely.

He stood up. All fear was gone. Before he realized what he was doing, he had moved toward her, meeting her in the middle of the walkway. Taking her in his arms, he kissed her, not waiting for permission, not caring what she thought or felt. He needed her, needed this. Wanted her for his own.

And she did not pull away.

"Adriana," he whispered.

"Edwin, what are we doing?" she asked.

"I couldn't let you go without seeing you one last time. Without Bethany."

She laughed softly. "Bethany would not approve of this," she said without releasing her embrace. "You and I are supposed to be friends. You promised."

"I am your friend, Adriana." He pressed his forehead against hers.

She sighed. "Do you kiss all your friends?"

"Yes," he teased. "Yes, I do."

He kissed her again. She clung to him, clutching his curls in her hand.

When she pulled back, she tenderly touched his

cheek with her fingers.

Just friends, she says. I don't believe her.

They sat down on the bench, silent, peaceful. The sun had begun its plunge behind the trees, causing the leaves to glimmer, green and gold. She nestled her head against him and he rested his chin on her dark head. They twined their fingers together, as if that alone would keep them from parting.

We fit together perfectly. Why should we be separated?

"Don't go," he said into her hair.

"You know I can't stay," she replied, gently rubbing her thumb against the hand that held hers.

"Sometimes we have to do difficult things we don't want to do," she said quietly. "We sacrifice for the common good."

Edwin's brow furrowed, wondering if the speech was intended to convince him or herself. "But isn't there some way—" he began.

"Shh. Don't talk. I want to remember us like this. Uncomplicated."

He sighed and breathed in the scent that was her.

Vanilla and cinnamon and roses.

He wasn't sure how long they sat there, together, unified, but suddenly she roused herself.

"I have to go," she said regretfully.

He was surprised to see how dark it had become.

A sliver of moon spied on them through the gaps in the canopy.

She sighed, studying his face as if trying to memorize it.

"We should never have met," she said quietly.

"Don't say that," he said. "You're the best thing that's ever happened to me."

"Don't say that," she said, shaking her head. They both stood, looking at each other. She took both his hands in hers. There were tears in her eyes as she looked up at him.

"Goodbye, Edwin Sterling."

So final.

He tried to say the words, but they stuck in his throat.

She turned to go. As she let go of his hands, he held one tightly, pulling her back to him. Once again, she did not resist, but returned his kiss passionately.

"I have to go," she said again, pulling away. This time she was successful.

"Goodbye," he said as she became one with the shadows.

For now.

14

She left. The day she left, the temperature dropped, as if she had taken the summer with her. They had promised to email each other. They had promised to call. But the emptiness was overwhelming.

Edwin was still in bed when Phillip stopped by. He grumbled out to the kitchen in his robe and drank his tea with a scowl on his face.

I told you so. That's what he's going to say.

"Well," Phillip began. Edwin literally growled at him.

"It's not my fault you started a relationship with someone from another country," his friend argued.

Edwin stared sullenly out of the window. The sky seemed white-washed, and the fog hung heavily over the grass as if it, too, was having a hard time rising.

Can't clear my head.

"Look," Phillip said, "there's something I wanted to ask you about. Remember when you went to Kensington?"

Edwin forced himself to look his way, but said nothing.

"There was a bomb threat nearby. Same day. Remember?"

"Yes."

"Well, interestingly enough," Phillip said, scratching his head, "it was the same guy."

"I know. Jen mentioned it."

"Ahmet Tastan, from Kara Inci," Phillip continued, as if he hadn't heard him. "Someone tried to kill him again. This time it was with a bomb."

"And it failed again."

"Yes. It failed."

"I had tea with him yesterday," announced Edwin suddenly, hoping to catch his friend off-guard. It worked.

"You did?"

"Yes. At the Museum. I—happened to be there."

"What did he say?" asked Phillip.

"He talked about raising his brother's children and carrying on his father's legacy."

Phillip nodded. "I hope he gets the opportunity," he said. "I hope he's safer at home. I suppose he told you he was leaving the country last night."

"He never mentioned it," Edwin said, glancing at his friend.

Why do I feel scrutinized?

"What are you trying to say?" he asked.

"I don't know," Phillip replied. "I guess I'm thinking that it sounds rather coincidental. Adriana shows up—"

"What could Adriana have to do with it?" Edwin snapped.

I hate him.

"She shows up, and there are two attempts on this guy's life. Then he leaves, and lo and behold, she leaves, too. Before she planned to, I might add. Maybe it's just a coincidence, but—"

"Of course it's a coincidence. What else could it be?"

I don't hate him, but I really, really despise him.

Phillip sat at the table, chin in hand, with a puzzled look on his face. "I don't know. I just don't know. It's weird, though. You have to admit that."

Edwin did admit it, but not aloud. She was a mysterious woman, but surely—surely she couldn't hide that? If she were the type of woman who kills oil magnates, wouldn't it be obvious? Wouldn't there be some sign? Some warning? Or is she a fantastic actress? No. I won't let you in my head, Phillip.

He closed his eyes and conjured up the image of Adriana coming toward him in the Cradle Walk. Once again he caught her in his arms and kissed her. No, she's not a killer.

She's perfect.

"I had dinner with my parents tonight," Edwin told Adriana. He had used all restraint and waited to call her until her second day home.

"Please give them my regards," she replied.

"I wish you could tell them in person."

There was silence on the other end of the phone.

Stupid. Don't make her feel guilty for leaving.

"I forgot to tell you," he said, changing the subject, "I spoke with Mr. Tastan the other day. At the Museum, after you had to leave."

"Oh!" she said, surprised. "What did you talk about?"

"Life. Death. Not being afraid. He's a remarkable man. He made quite an impression on me. If he is all he says he is."

"I see."

"I can't help wondering why someone's trying to kill him."

"It's none of our concern, is it?"

"No? His would-be killer fell at my feet. How can I not be concerned?"

Adriana sighed. "Why should I care about Mr. Tastan?"

"I don't know," said Edwin, somewhat crestfallen. "I thought you'd want to help me solve the mystery."

"This is real life, Edwin. It's dangerous to get involved in things you know so little about. It's safer to stay out of it. Besides," she went on, "I don't have time to worry about a Turkish man with a death threat."

"Back to work, right?"

"Yes."

She paused.

"Now that I'm home, I won't have much time for—well, I just need to concentrate on my work. Not be distracted, you know? I hope you won't be offended if I'm not always available."

"No. No, of course not," Edwin lied. "You have a job to do."

Friendship only. Again.

15

Edwin found that the agreed-upon "friendship only" relationship with Adriana was easier to maintain from a great distance, at least on the surface level. He had even begun to convince himself that he could handle taking a minor role in her life, as long as he had a role.

It took several weeks for life to return to normal, at least normal for Edwin Sterling. Jen came every Monday to talk about the coming week; Debra continued to bother him about film scripts, hoping to tempt him with the next potential blockbuster; David constantly coaxed him into charity events and talk show appearances. Edwin also felt pulled by events not required of him, like a former costar's movie premiere or an art gallery opening by one of his mother's friends.

"Edwin, we'd love to have you for this."

"Edwin, couldn't you do us this one favor?"

"Edwin, it just wouldn't be the same without you there."

Always on display.

He had forgotten what it felt like to be normal.

Really normal. Unknown. Forgotten. Like at the mixers at school when the boys' school invited the girls' school to a dance. Phillip was always the popular one, the guy all the girls wanted to dance with, to sneak out behind the rhododendron hedge and kiss. That was normal for Phillip. Normal for Edwin was to haunt the refreshments table and go to the bathroom every fifteen minutes, just to give himself an excuse to be out of the room.

A shy theatre boy with a case of acne was not what the girls were after. He only ever felt normal on the stage; he gained confidence pretending to be someone else.

It was safer to play a role.

Now he couldn't even enter a room without being recognized. He was known as confident, witty, gallant Dr. Hanover, universally adored by every unmarried female on both sides of the Atlantic.

Except for Adriana.

Maybe Phillip was right. Maybe there is another man.

Just like Mary Alice Rowan.

"Would you like to dance, Edwin?" Mary Alice had asked.

"Me?" he had responded, looking around. Surely not me. At fifteen, Edwin had been two or three inches shorter than his current six feet, and ridiculously skinny. Mary Alice was the prettiest girl at Holy Trinity.

"Yes, you, silly!" she had said, taking his hand.

Edwin had felt so proud, so important. The other guys watched in awe as Mary Alice led him to the dance floor. She even gave him her parents' phone number and said he could call her. She said she wanted to come see him in his theatre production. He remembered the times he had called her, awkwardly trying to sound grown up and respectful when her father answered the phone. She always seemed slightly aloof in those conversations. Polite, but somewhat distant. Edwin had convinced himself that she was being more guarded because her parents were listening.

She came the last night of the show and stayed for the cast party afterward. Edwin remembered being awkwardly pleased with himself; Mary Alice had worn a beautiful dress and shiny lip gloss. She seemed to like him, laughing at his attempts at jokes and complimenting his performance. His head was in the clouds. One of the other boys suggested he take her behind the rhododendron bushes behind the school, the ultimate destination for a secret rendezvous. He was surprised when she agreed to go with him.

It was dark in the rhododendrons, with only a patchwork of light that filtered through the branches from the street lamps. Mary Alice was more of a shadow than a real person in front of him.

Like a dream.

He only knew she was real because of her perfume.

She smelled like Anais Anais.

He felt stupidly self-conscious as he lunged at her face, his lips puckered. His stomach quivered with fear and anticipation. He tentatively put his hands around her waist, unsure if that was where he was supposed to put them.

Her lipgloss tasted like strawberries.

Mary Alice wrapped her arms around his neck, as if she were holding on for dear life. It made him feel masculine, needed, wanted. It made him feel like a man.

After the kiss, they stumbled out of the bushes, blinking at the brightness of the street lamps in the parking lot. His heart was doing somersaults against his ribcage.

They went back inside the green room; he felt triumphant. All the boys knew where they'd been, that he had kissed Mary Alice Rowan.

That's when Mary Alice saw Stephen Quinn.

"Isn't that Stephen Quinn?" she had asked him.

"Yeah," he had replied. Stephen was two years

older. Stephen had well-developed muscles. Stephen didn't have acne. Stephen was the son of an Irish peer.

"Can you introduce us?" she had asked. "I want to tell him he did a great job tonight."

Edwin had introduced them. That's when she asked him to get her some punch. While he was away, presumably, she had given Stephen her parents' phone number. She had told him he could call her.

The next week, when he called Mary Alice to ask her to go to the movies, she already had a date with Stephen.

"Let's just be friends, Edwin," she had said, in a bright, happy-sounding voice. As if she'd never considered him in any other light. As if she'd never kissed him behind the rhododendron bushes. "I don't like you *that* way, Edwin."

It had been a crushing blow at the time. Edwin had cried himself to sleep many nights afterward. The most humiliating part about it was that everyone had known. It was the kind of wound a teenaged boy would never forget.

It was the kind of wound a grown man felt freshly, as if it had just happened, even when he hadn't thought about it in years.

16

It was Tuesday, and Edwin was trying to avoid a particularly irritating phone request from David.

"Hey, man, was wondering if you'd be willing to
be the celebrity date for this Breast Cancer Awareness
auction coming up. All you have to do is agree to go
to dinner in a pink limo with some lucky rich girl
whose parents want to donate money. What do you
say? Call me back."

Edwin immediately left the house, turned off his
phone, and headed to the last place David would ever
venture into.

The British Museum.

And this time, he did wear the hat.

Bypassing the cuneiform tablets, he went directly
to the Egyptian exhibit, filled with huge hieroglyphics
and massive pieces of ancient tombs. No one seemed
to notice him. At least, not yet.

For a long time, he stood in front of the enormous
head of Rameses II. It brought pedestals again to
his mind. This carved head would have stood tow-
ering above the people, a testament of the Pharaoh's

greatness, a symbol of his power. Edwin knew that to modern thought, the idea of divine right of kings was passé, snickered at behind closed university doors. The Pharaohs were considered arrogant tyrants. But looking up at the stone face in front of him, he wondered what kind of man he had really been. What does it take to rule a nation?

From experience, he knew that sometimes people of prominence don't always climb onto the pedestals of their own accord. Sometimes they are placed there at the insistence of those around them. People looking for something, or someone, to worship.

But pedestals are also easy targets.

His thoughts soon turned from Egyptian pharaohs to Turkish oil magnates. This is where it had all happened a few weeks ago. A shot in the dark catwalks above his head. Despite Adriana's warning to keep out of it, he couldn't help wanting to go back to where the first attack on Ahmet Tastan had taken place.

The Arched Room.

There were two other occupants of the room when he entered. Edwin ignored them; their heads were bowed over a cuneiform tablet.

The room was even more impressive without a crowd. As he stood in awe at the rows and rows of books and documents lining the walls of the room, he tried to remember all the details of that day.

He stood lost in thought at the front end of the room where Mr. Tastan had stood that day. He gazed unseeingly above the heads of the two students to where the shooter, with his tripod gun, had stood on the catwalk.

One of the students stood up and came toward him.

"Edwin Sterling?" she asked.

Edwin's eyes focused on the speaker. Her flyaway blond hair and her nondescript clothes pulled on his memory.

"Bethany?"

"I thought that was you. Almost didn't recognize you because of the hat. What are you doing here?"

Edwin didn't know how to explain himself.

Why am I really here?

"Just visiting the museum," he explained with a shrug.

She's not buying it.

Bethany adjusted her glasses.

"You want to reenact the scene," she said.

Edwin scratched the back of his neck. "I was in the neighborhood, and I thought I'd just come in and—yes, take another look."

Bethany appraised him from behind her glasses. Edwin was surprised to find her so alarmingly intense and serious. He had thought her absent-minded when they first met, kind of a muddleheaded book-worm with an overprotective streak. The Bethany standing before him now was clearheaded and stern, almost aloof, as she looked at him.

Uncomfortable. A little scary.

She seemed to make up her mind.

"You aren't really allowed in here. Technically, this area isn't open to the public, except during special events. But, okay. I'll play along."

"The shooter never took a shot because someone shot him," began Edwin.

"Yes. From up here." She indicated an upper gallery toward the middle of the room. "The second shooter shot from here in the middle toward the shooter in the back of the room."

"And killed him, which protected Mr. Tastan. Who was he? The man who almost fell on me, I mean."

She shrugged. "His enemy, I presume."

Edwin grinned. "And whatever happened to the second shooter? I never saw him at all."

"Disappeared."

"How is that even possible?" asked Edwin, gazing up at the upper gallery. "With a room full of people? No one saw him?"

Bethany shrugged again. "There was a lot of chaos.

After you said there was a gun, everyone in the room hit the floor. No one was looking up. It would be easy to escape."

"Were you here?" Edwin asked. "I didn't see you or Adriana that day."

"Of course I was here. I work in this department."

"Huh. I guess I didn't realize that."

"You know you're not really Dr. Hanover, right?" she asked.

"Yeah, I know," Edwin said, rolling his eyes. He gazed up again at the upper gallery, frowning in thought.

Bethany blinked a few times, watching him.

"Adriana needs to concentrate right now," she said, seemingly out of the blue, her head on one side. "She can't be distracted."

"She told me," he said, trying not to show any emotion.

"It doesn't seem to me like you're making it easy for her."

She looked like an owl, with her eyes magnified by her glasses. A blond, frizzy-headed owl.

Owls are wise.

Owls are predatory.

Edwin shifted his footing so she wouldn't notice his involuntary shudder.

"Easy for her?" he asked. "It seems to be infinitely

easy for her. I'm the one who—"

"Who what?"

"Wants more."

He met her owl-like stare. She blinked.

"Be a good friend," she said, turning back to her student and the cuneiform tablet.

Edwin sat impatiently at his computer, logged into Skype. Waiting. Always waiting. Staring at this stupid screen, waiting for the incredibly beautiful sound that showed Adriana was online.

It had been three months since Adriana left England. Three months of hurried phone calls with a seven-hour time difference, waiting until after midnight to catch her right before work, or trying to be available if she called at the end of her day, which was the middle of his. This was particularly difficult now that his work schedule had picked up. Three weeks of filming a movie in Scotland, much to Debra's delight, as well as several film festival appearances, had taken their toll. Emails were more reliable and more frequent, but still left so many things unsaid. Be a good friend, Bethany had said. But Edwin longed to know every detail of Adriana's life, not just what she chose to tell him, and he wished he could share every detail of his with her.

He was thankful, though, that there was a friendship.

When Mary Alice had asked to be friends, what she really wanted was for him to stop calling. What she really wanted was for him to step quietly out of the picture.

Back to the sidelines.

Back to the refreshments table and the frequent bathroom trips.

But Adriana didn't seem to want that. When they were able to talk, they talked like they had in England, about literature, about art, about current events.

But not about their relationship.

Not about us.

Edwin's mind wandered as he waited for her to call. His favorite times were weekends, when they could Skype and he could see her beautiful face again. Even then, Adriana wasn't always available. He feared it was purposeful.

What does she do when she can't Skype? And with whom?

Occasionally, Edwin used the Find My Friends app on his phone to see if he could figure out where she was.

Is that technically stalking?

Jen said it was, but it never revealed anything startling. Back and forth to work, the occasional restaurant. Of course, it didn't show him who she was with.

A nameless, faceless man still loomed in Edwin's

imagination, standing in the way of his intimacy with Adriana. A man like Stephen Quinn.

Maybe I should plan a visit.

In his mind, he saw Adriana walking toward him again in the Cradle Walk. He rose to meet her, taking her in his arms. But she was speaking, not returning his embrace. The lurking fear wafted over him like it had for a brief moment in Kensington.

"Edwin, I've been lying to you. There's someone else, and he's so much better than you—"

Edwin's mental whirling came to a halt when he heard the familiar sound of a Skype call coming in. He wiped his forehead with his hand.

Stay in reality.

"I wasn't sure you'd call today," he said after answering.

"Sorry," she replied. "Time got away from me."

He tried not to look crestfallen.

I'm not important enough to make time for.

"Look," she began, "I can't talk long now. I'm actually kind of busy. Something's come up. Work and all."

"Of course," he said as his heart sank to his knees.

Here it comes.

"But, I—I have good news. At least, I think it's good news. Remember how I said I couldn't come for your birthday celebration next week?"

"Yes. How could I forget?"

"Well, it turns out, I can come after all."

She smiled shyly, looking up at him on the computer screen.

"Edwin?"

"Yes?"

"You're silent. Should I not come?"

"No! I mean, yes, please come! Sorry, I—was just so surprised. I thought you were going to say something else."

"Like what?"

"Never mind. I would love for you to come."

"I'm staying with Bethany."

"Of course."

Bethany, my biggest fan.

Adriana paused.

"Edwin?"

"Yes?"

"I can't wait to see you again."

He caught his breath, but tried to act nonchalant.

Be a good friend.

"It'll be good—yes, I—I'm so glad you'll be able to come. It means a lot to me."

"I know."

17

He didn't always have a big to-do, but this was a mile-stone birthday. Thirty-five.

Man, I'm old.

Although he rarely checked, Edwin knew he was mentioned in the media just about daily. Fortunately, since Adriana had left England, it had been months since the topic was his mystery girlfriend. With a new film under his belt and the next season of *Dr. Hanover* soon to begin rehearsals, that subject had been pushed to the back of the internet's mind. But his birthday, he knew, would bring it to the forefront. Photographers would snap pictures of him and his guests, and reporters would inevitably ask the question he didn't know how to answer:

'Is this your mystery girlfriend?'

He knew Adriana had arrived in England because she had texted him. Also, her blip on Find My Friends showed she had crossed the ocean.

Definitely not stalking.

He had decided to have his celebration at Début, the not-so-new-now first restaurant of the acclaimed chef, Pierre Ferrar. It had delicious food and ample room for guests and dancing. Plus, he loved that it was housed in a former Victorian department store with plenty of architectural romance and a roof garden for outdoor ambience.

All of his friends, family, and colleagues had been invited, and quite a few hangers-on he didn't really like but felt compelled to invite. He knew that, like most of the parties he had thrown or attended, there would be additional "guests" brought as special favors by actual guests to advance their careers. He also knew that less than half of the party-goers would be there to genuinely wish him well. Most would only be there to be seen, by him or others. Thinking about being constantly "on" exhausted him already.

But Adriana will be there.

"Is she here yet?"

Phillip nudged his friend.

"Not yet."

"You seem a little preoccupied," Phillip continued. "Staring at the door. Your parents just got here."

Edwin sighed and shook himself out of his reverie. Got to stay focused on my guests.

"Many happy returns, darling!" his mother said, kissing his cheek. His father patted him good-naturedly on the arm.

"Thanks."

"Should we be expecting Adriana?" asked his mother.

"Any moment now."

She seemed pleased. His father frowned.

"I thought you said she wouldn't be able to come?"

"Last minute change. Her schedule freed up."

"Hmm." Sir Thomas looked thoughtful, his eyebrows lowering over his eyes.

Odd. Thought he liked her.

Brenda, Phillip's wife, approached the group.

"I can't wait to meet her, Ed," she said excitedly. "Oh, and many happy returns!"

"Thanks, Brenda."

"What's the name of that blonde over there?" she asked. "The one talking to your director friend. She's that American pop singer, isn't she?"

Edwin glanced in the direction she indicated. A pretty blonde with bright red lipstick and wearing an extremely short, tight dress wiggled her fingers at him.

"Chloe," he said, turning back to Brenda.

"That's it. I didn't know you knew her?"

"I don't."

"Well," said Brenda, "Adriana better watch out. I think Chloe is out to get you!"

Edwin forced himself to mingle with his guests, but couldn't keep his eyes off the door.

She's not coming. Something happened to scare her off.

He had sent his driver, Bill, for them in the car. They should be here by now. Suddenly, his pocket vibrated. It was a text from Bethany.

She won't come in. Feels in the spotlight.

I'm coming out, he replied.

No! Much worse. Let me handle it.

Jen meandered over, her new husband, Gerald, on her arm.

"Great party, Edwin!" she said.

"Thanks to you," he agreed, kissing her on the cheek. He shook Gerald's hand.

Jen gave a dramatic glance around the room.

"I see David, and Debra, and your parents and lots and lots of friends. Am I missing your one particular friend?" she asked sarcastically.

"She'll be here."

She leaned in close.

"David and Debra are at it again," she whispered. "They're driving me crazy!"

"This is a birthday party, not a film festival. You're not on duty. Just ignore them," he said.

"I'll try to stay out of their sight," she said.

She grinned her girlish smile at him as they

moved on.

"Edwin!" His costar, Genevieve Boyd, kissed him on each cheek. "I brought you a present!"

She pressed a bottle of wine into his hands.

"Thank you, Genevieve," he replied. He noticed Genevieve looked stunning in a long, red, backless gown, her meticulously-coiffed blonde hair swept across one eye in a style reminiscent of old movie stars.

Always looking for the photo op, Edwin thought, amused.

"How's John?" he asked.

"Splendid," she replied. "He's over at the bar, talking politics with poor Harry!" Harry played Dr. Hanover's sidekick and fellow doctor on the show.

Edwin frowned sympathetically in Harry's direction. Genevieve's husband, John, was known to climb onto his political soapbox after a few glasses of wine. He could just overhear a few snippets of their conversation.

"And that's why allowing these Middle Eastern nations to supply our oil is foolish," John was declaring, stabbing Harry in the chest with his forefinger as he spoke.

"But we need oil, don't we? We have to get it from somewhere," argued Harry.

"Peat," John said. "And coal. We can go back to

the old ways."

"But I can't put peat in my car!" Harry protested.

Edwin shook his head and checked his phone again. No texts. And no Adriana.

Genevieve noticed his nervous actions.

"Mystery girlfriend a no-show?" she asked.

Edwin could feel his cheeks burn as they colored.

Why do I have to blush so easily?

"Yet to be seen," he replied.

He set his wine bottle down on a nearby table and started to move toward the door, but was stopped short by a dramatic, heavily braceleted arm.

"Edwin Sterling? I just had to come and wish you a Happy Birthday!"

It was Chloe. She batted her false eyelashes at him and pouted her red mouth.

"Thank you," said Edwin.

"Simon was such a *darling*! When I heard he was coming to your birthday party tonight, I absolutely *insisted* he bring me along! I've wanted to meet you for *so* long! I'm such a *Dr. Hanover* fan!"

"Well, again, thank you," Edwin said politely, looking over her shoulder toward the door.

Please come in, Adriana.

"You know," Chloe lowered her voice to a sultry purr, "I'll be in town for several weeks while I'm re-cording my next record. I'd *love* to get to know the real Edwin Sterling. Maybe we can get together for lunch—or dinner. I'm staying at the Ace—"

"Pardon me. Sorry." He pushed past her.

Edwin had stopped listening about halfway through her flirtatious speech. Adriana had finally appeared at the door.

Chloe stared after him as he crossed the room, her red mouth half open in surprise.

Edwin couldn't take his eyes off Adriana as he pushed through the crowd. She stood just inside the large mahogany doors, nervously glancing around the room.

Looking for me.

Début's signature Victorian staircase descended in a wide sweep about ten steps from the front doors to the main room below. Edwin rushed up them, eager to reach her before she changed her mind.

She was a vision in silver; she shimmered like a star. But it was Bethany he greeted first.

"Thank you," he whispered as he kissed Bethany's cheek. "For everything."

Bethany nodded her head, her owl-like eyes dropping shyly to the ground. She had dressed up for the occasion and was even wearing makeup.

"Happy Birthday, Edwin," said Adriana, her eyes shining.

He offered her his arm. No kiss. Nothing to embarrass her. He offered his other arm to Bethany.

His sudden movement across the room had drawn some attention. As they descended the staircase, he could see his mother's beaming expression, and he could just make out Brenda's "She's lovely!" as she excitedly grabbed Phillip's arm.

Chloe's red pout was even more pouty than before. She folded her arms and glowered as Adriana was enthusiastically greeted by Edwin's friends and family.

He could hear whispers in the crowd: Who is she? Do you know her? It wouldn't be long before they figured out that this was the same woman from the summer.

Let them talk.

Adriana and Brenda seemed to get along well from the start. Edwin was pleased to see the two women talking and laughing together. Later, Brenda cornered him at one of the buffet tables.

"Oh, Edwin! She's perfect for you!"

"I'm glad you agree," he said gratefully.

"I wish Phillip agreed. He kept interrogating her. Asked about her family, where she grew up. And he kept asking her about her work, whether they were okay with her taking time off. He even asked her questions about her particular museum and the area she curates. It was weird, like he'd studied up on it or something. Like he thought she was hiding something."

"What did he decide? Is she hiding something?"

Brenda shrugged. "You'll have to ask him. I gave him the evil eye to make him stop."

Edwin glanced across to where Phillip stood talking with a group of friends. Why can't he just be happy for me?

"Adriana, this is my publicist, David," said Edwin.

"Finally! The Mystery Woman in the flesh!" David said, eyeing her up and down. She smiled nervously.

Edwin touched the back of Adriana's arm in a "back off, David" kind of way.

"So you're the one who finally brought truth to my rumors," David went on.

"Of course, Edwin and I are just good friends," Adriana explained.

"Of course," said David with a wink.

"Hold on," said Edwin. "Did you just say "my rumors"?"

David's smile froze momentarily.

"Did I?" he asked, searching the room for a way of escape.

"Yes, I believe you did," Edwin said, holding on to his arm.

"Well, it worked, didn't it? I mean, it was just

good publicity fun.   And you were so concerned about not being able to meet a woman. I thought if everyone thought you were already taken, they'd leave you alone, and you'd be free to meet someone. And you did!"

"A lunatic almost killed her because of your lies!"

"But she didn't, did she?" David wheedled. "Your mystery woman has a few tricks up her sleeve! It all worked out." He shrugged.

Edwin could feel the rage surging through his face. His fists were clenched as he glared at his publicist.

Adriana put a light hand on his arm.

"Let it go," she said soothingly.   "It's not worth fighting over. What's done is done."

"Yeah, Edwin," David joined in. "What's done is done."

She turned an intimidating gaze on him, and he quickly crossed the room to flirt with Genevieve.

18

Pierre Ferrar had designed an elaborate cake for the event. When it was time to cut it, the famous chef stood beside his masterpiece, smiling proudly. "Happy Birthday" was sung, loudly and out of tune. Edwin was asked to cut the first slice, and he obediently did. There was a lot of laughter and camera flashes and well-wishes. As Edwin looked around afterward, however, he noticed that Adriana had stayed toward the back of the group. She was there, clapping, smiling at him, but she was definitely trying to blend into the crowd and not stand out. She seemed determined to stay out of the photographs. Their eyes met. Fear again, despite her smiles. And something else.

Sadness?

While the cake was being served, Edwin felt like he was in a sea of well-wishers and birthday greetings; every time one wave passed, another came. He was afraid he was neglecting Adriana, so he was relieved when he saw his father hand her a piece of cake and stay to make conversation. He was too far away to eavesdrop, but he was struck again by his father's odd manner toward her. He seemed somewhat gruff, not angry, but not his usual diplomatic self. Her response to him was like a child with her father; her eyes were mostly downcast as she listened to him, but he did sense a bit of her temper flaring at times.

Maybe it's an American thing?

The waves had ebbed for a moment, so he began moving toward her, slowly and deliberately. He hadn't gotten very far when a hand grabbed his arm.

"Dance with me, Edwin Sterling!"

Chloe was pulling him toward her.

"Sorry," he said, "I've already got a partner."

He reached out and took Adriana's hand. "Dance with me," he whispered urgently. Sir Thomas smiled a reluctant blessing on them and tried to offer his own hand to Chloe, who pretended not to notice and turned her back.

Guests parted the way for them as they headed for the dance floor. Others joined them, eager for fun. Chloe scowled after them, her hands on her hips.

"Was that Chloe?" Adriana asked, raising her eyebrows.

"Yes, I'm afraid so. Just met her tonight. She came with a friend."

Adriana grimaced. "I'm afraid we may find ourselves in her next song."

"Not really?" Edwin asked, smothering a laugh. "Well, so be it."

A slow song was playing. Edwin took her in his arms, but kept a respectful distance between them.

Don't push your luck. Not yet.

As they danced, Adriana glanced around the room. Although there was the constant chatter of friends or buttering up of betters, there were also quite a few guests surrounding the dance floor or sitting idly at tables, watching.

"What's the matter?" Edwin asked.

Adriana shrugged her shoulders. "I'm a little uncomfortable being watched."

"You are dancing with the birthday boy," he reminded her.

She smiled. Her eyes circled the room again as they danced.

"Chloe is definitely trying to cast an evil spell on us. But she's not the only one. Edwin, why do I feel like every woman in the room wants to kill me?"

"Are you really afraid of that happening again? Surely it was a once-in-a-lifetime experience, despite David's best efforts. Although, he's right. You do have a few tricks up your sleeve. You could probably take down any woman here. Or any man."

"Wrong choice of words, perhaps. But really, Edwin, many of them are looking at me like I'm their worst enemy."

Edwin looked down into her face. Her hazel eyes were dazzling; the silver of her dress brought out gray and gold specks in them.

"Because you're the one I'm dancing with," he said simply. "You're the one I chose."

He could see the truth finally settle into her mind.

"So they think we're together. The Mystery Girlfriend in the flesh. And they're jealous of me."

Edwin nodded.

"Well, that's simple to solve," she said. "You just have to explain to them that we're just friends. That I'm not a threat. Or get your publicist to do it," she said with a coy smile.

Edwin shook his head. "It's too late."

"Why?"

"Because your face is inextricably linked to mine."

"Because of the internet?"

"Afraid so. And even if it weren't, Adriana," he said, pulling her close and whispering in her ear, "You are the most beautiful woman in the room tonight. The eyes of every man are on you. Including mine. I'm afraid you are very much a threat."

They danced on, cheek to cheek now. He couldn't see her face, but he could feel her heart beating close to his and he could hear her breath quicken in his ear.

I'm winning.

The song ended. Edwin pulled her toward the staircase that led to the roof.

"Come with me."

The roof garden was secluded and romantic, reserved for special occasions and special guests. Edwin hoped no one else had had the same idea, to come up there.

It was wonderfully empty.

"Wow!" Adriana gasped, admiring the view. "Edwin, this is lovely!"

The cool, September night was refreshing after the warm room below. They could see the rooftops and chimneys of an older section of London, with the newer, more modern buildings reflecting the streetlights in the distance. Behind them, herbs, lavender and roses were interspersed with urns of chrysanthemums in wild colors, begging for autumn's arrival.

He stood beside her and looked out across the city.

I'm proud to live here, he thought. I'm proud to be standing here next to her.

"There's no one around," he said.

"No," she agreed cautiously.

"No paparazzi. No angry pop stars. No mothers."

She laughed.

Making progress.

"No Bethany."

"Oh! Bethany!" she cried, stricken that she had

left her friend alone.

"No Bethany!" he repeated, pulling her closer.

"No Bethany," she said, relaxing a little.

"Thank you for being here," he said.

She nodded. "I'm glad I was able to come. This is a great party."

He agreed. "Jen did a nice job pulling it all together. But, there's one thing missing."

"Oh?"

"Yes. Something I really want, but no one's given me yet."

"What is it?"

"A birthday kiss."

She narrowed her eyes. "I've seen many women give you a kiss tonight. Some of them on both cheeks!"

"Yes," he agreed, "but that isn't what I was looking for."

"No?" she asked.

"No. Because it wasn't from you."

She reached up and planted a playful kiss on his cheek.

He shook his head. "Almost. But not quite. Although you do smell delicious."

"I think it's those rose bushes."

"Oh."

He watched her face as she made up her mind.

She smiled up at him. "Happy Birthday, Edwin Sterling," she said. Then she kissed him softly on the mouth.

He pretended to consider it.

"Was that what you were looking for?" she asked.

"I think so. Maybe you should do it again, just to be sure."

She obeyed.

"Yes. That was it."

He pressed his cheek against hers. Soft and smooth. Like velvet. Another reason why—

"I love you."

He froze. *What did I say?*

"What?" she whispered.

"Nothing. I—"

He could hear voices coming up the stairs. No longer alone. *Thank God!*

Maybe she'll forget what I said.

Edwin nearly dragged Adriana down the stairs to the party below. His mind was reeling.

What have I done? I'm such a fool, to say those words. Do I even mean them?

He looked over at her. Adriana's face seemed flushed, but she didn't look angry. *Maybe she didn't hear it.*

Bethany had not been neglected; she was having a

lively conversation with Genevieve's husband, John.

"Peat moss?" he heard her say. "That's your solution?"

"We've got to return to the old ways. A self-sufficient Britain is a free Britain," said John.

"Why don't we go the whole way, then?" suggested Bethany. "Horses and buggies again. Like the Amish. Then we wouldn't need oil at all."

John waved a drunken finger in her face. "You've got a point there, young lady," he said.

When Bethany noticed Adriana, she turned into the over-protective owl again. Edwin could feel her staring holes into his brain with her magnified laser-eyes. Although she appeared calm on the surface, Edwin sensed that Adriana had once again gone into a defense-mode of coolness toward him.

I'll make it up to her tomorrow. We can talk this out.

Do I love her?

At the end of the evening, Edwin walked them out to the waiting car. As Bethany got into the vehicle, he pulled Adriana aside.

"Again, thank you so much for coming."

"I'm glad I could be here."

"So, I'll call you tomorrow. We can have lunch or something."

Adriana's body stiffened noticeably.

"I'm actually leaving in the morning," she explained.

"In the morning? But you just got here!"

"I know, but—"

"But I thought you'd be staying the whole weekend? I hoped to spend more time together."

"I'm sorry, Edwin. I know you're disappointed, and I don't expect you to understand. There are things I have to do."

She moved toward the car.

He could see Bethany leaning forward in the back seat, looking protectively owl-like. For the first time, he noticed the flashes and the click of cameras around him.

And he didn't care.

"You're just leaving, then. With no explanation? Did I do something wrong?" he asked. He hadn't meant to speak so snappishly, but he didn't apologize.

She stopped. "I planned this, to leave tomorrow. I just didn't tell you before because I wanted you to focus on your birthday party."

"Well, Happy Birthday to me!" he said loudly and sarcastically.

"Edwin!" It was his mother's voice, scolding him from the door of the restaurant.

"Can we at least talk about this when you get

home?" he asked.

"I'm not going home," she said, visibly restless. "I need to—be alone right now. You won't be able to get in touch with me for awhile."

"How long?"

She clenched her fist. "I don't know." She looked at him defiantly, like a caged animal.

Anger began to build inside him.

She's just like Mary Alice.

He stepped closer. "What's his name?" he asked.

"Whose name?"

"The man who stands between you and me."

She glared at him.

"Right now, his name is Edwin Sterling."

"Fine." He shook his head, throwing up his hands. "You know what, I don't care. Just cut me off."

"It's just for now, Edwin."

"Adriana," Bethany warned.

She shook her head, her eyes squeezed shut. "I have to go."

She climbed into the back seat. Edwin's driver, Bill, shut the door. He appeared uncomfortable, tugging on the brim of his hat, but he got into the driver's seat and pulled away, leaving Edwin standing on the sidewalk.

Flash.

He squinted and put up a hand to shield his face as

cameras flashed around him.

Gone in a flash.

19

The rest of the night moved in fast-forward. Outside, there were questions: Having a domestic, Edwin? Was that your Mystery Woman? Is it all over between you? He pushed past them without a word.

I have nothing to say.

Inside wasn't any better. David was angry.

"If you're going to have a lovers' quarrel, have it indoors!" he said, dragging him back inside the restaurant. "I know you're angry with me about this whole 'mystery woman' thing, but for God's sake, Edwin! Can't you think?"

He was irritated by his mother's remarks about giving Adriana breathing room, not moving too fast. Not scaring her off. His father was the most puzzling. He looked stern and serious. More than once Edwin thought he was going to say something to him, but Sir Thomas never did. Phillip and Brenda and Jen and Gerald all tried to carry on as usual, with falsely bright, smiling faces and counterfeit laughter, as if nothing had happened at all.

The next morning, when he woke up on his sofa

still in his clothes, he found a note in flowery script in his pocket. It had Chloe's phone number and "See you tomorrow" on it. He had a vague memory of her cuddling up next to him, but he couldn't remember what he'd promised to do. Lunch, maybe?

I don't care.

The last time she left, it felt like Adriana had taken summer with her. This time it felt to Edwin like she had taken the sun itself. His mind was a dark blankness. He lay on the sofa, staring up at the antique light fixture on the ceiling. He just wanted to sleep. To stay asleep and never wake again. What is life without Adriana?

Don't be ridiculous. You're not fifteen anymore. You're thirty-five years old. You value truth, right? And she's obviously keeping you in the dark.

Move on.

But Edwin couldn't move on. Not completely. He got out of bed. He went to rehearsals. He made appearances for charity events. And he did smile. And he did his best to avoid the questions. But it was hollow. Not real.

Acting.

Minutes after "the argument", pictures of him and Adriana were all over the internet. Gossip websites gleefully announced that Edwin Sterling was still available after all, to the delight of all his female fans. Some news sources vilified him for the argument, suggesting he had a volatile temper; some vilified the Mystery Woman. None of them, as yet, knew her name.

Brenda texted that afternoon, as Edwin found himself still lounging forlornly on his sofa.

Check out Chloe's Instagram account.

Chloe had posted a selfie of herself the night before, with Edwin in the background looking dazed and miserable. As a caption, she had written, "First date tomorrow. Dinner at Hoi Polloi at the Ace."

Edwin ran both hands through his hair and stood it up on end. Did I agree to that? He couldn't remember. But that would explain the note.

He glanced at the clock. Five-fifteen. He had taken a shower and changed his clothes that morning. That was all he'd accomplished that day.

He knew, with an announcement on Instagram, that Chloe meant for their date to be publicly known and paparazzi-reported.

Well, why not?

Adriana left, didn't she?

And we're just friends.

He looked at his phone again. Adriana. I should call. Just to see if she'll pick up.

The anger welled up in him again as he remembered all she'd said. He powered down his phone completely.

20

The Ace Hotel was in an area of London called Shoreditch. It was a boutique hotel that catered to the artistic community. Edwin could see why Chloe had chosen it for her London stay.

As he got out of the cab, he wasn't surprised to see a couple of photographers waiting to take his picture. What he didn't expect was the number of onlookers. Men in dark suits had formed a line of protection. He could hear his name called and hands reached out to him from across the arms of the security detail. He waved and smiled; the screaming that ensued from this seemingly simple action nearly deafened him.

He entered the Hoi Polloi restaurant, expecting Chloe to be there waiting for him. What he found was not only a crowd of Chloe's friends, but everyone in the restaurant, from the staff to the customers, seemed to be waiting for him.

Some first date.

"Edwin!" Chloe squealed when she saw him.

She leaped from her seat and gave him a dramatic kiss on the cheek.

"Oh! Sorry!" she said, wiping her lipstick mark off his face.

She was wearing a bright blue blouse with a colorful scarf knotted at her neck.

Never noticed how pretty she is.

In an overdone, glamorous kind of way.

She led him to another table, away from her friends. It had been laid for two.

Thank goodness.

"I thought we'd want to be alone," she said in a sultry whisper.

Alone to Chloe was across a crowded room full of people who were watching her every move, but Edwin was thankful for at least that much space.

"So," she began as they sat down,"how are you doing?"

"As well as can be expected," he responded with a bitter edge to his voice.

Chloe pouted her lips in an attempt at sympathy.

"Who is she? The girl you argued with?"

"A friend," said Edwin cautiously.

None of her business, really.

Chloe shrugged off all thoughts of Adriana.

"Well, we're here together now. I'll help put you in a better mood," she said, trying to sound seductive.

The fortuitous arrival of the waiter allowed Edwin to change the subject after they ordered.

"So, you're in town recording an album?" he asked. Edwin had never listened to Chloe's music. He silently hoped she wouldn't expect him to know any of her songs.

"Yes!" Chloe brightened immediately. "We start tomorrow. Bradford Harrow is producing it, you know."

Edwin nodded enthusiastically, making a mental note to look up the name later.

"It's going to be called *Queen of Everything*. Isn't that a great title? I've got a song with that title, too."

"Oh? What's it about?" asked Edwin.

"Me, of course," she answered, surprised. "So the gimmick is to write songs comparing me to, like, all the different queens and stuff, and so since there were so many in England, we thought coming here to record would be a fantastic idea."

"Oh!" said Edwin, not sure how to respond.

"I'm also going to visit historic places, you know, to get in the mood. Castles and stuff. And the Crown jewels. I hear they're so lovely! I'd love to wear them. I wonder if they'd let me? I'll have to ask my manager about that."

Edwin smiled weakly.

"Well, it sounds like quite an undertaking," he said.

"Yeah, I guess. But Bradford can do anything."

The waiter deposited a bottle of champagne on the table with two fluted glasses. Chloe batted her false eyelashes at Edwin as she reached across the table and grabbed his hand.

Photo op.

And flash.

"So," she said, pouring him champagne, "what's it like being Dr. Hanover? It must be so cool, solving all those crimes and stuff."

Edwin sighed.

I'm not Dr. Hanover.

"It's fun," he said, deciding to be tolerant. "A lot of work, but I love my costars and we really have a good time working together."

It's fiction. It's not real life.

"I've watched every episode. I'm *so* jealous of Sandra! That last episode when you kissed her, I thought I was gonna die! Marianne and Shelly were with me," she said, indicating two friends across the room who giggled and averted their eyes when Edwin glanced in their direction.

Sandra was Genevieve's character. There was an ongoing feud among *Dr. Hanover* fans; some wanted Dr. Hanover and Sandra, the feisty pathologist, to get together, and some were extremely jealous of her. Extremely.

"It caused quite a Twitter explosion, I hear," he said.

Fortunately, their appetizer came at just the right moment. Apparently, food was one of Chloe's favorite subjects.

When she wasn't discussing the various dishes from her favorite restaurants around the world, she was talking at length about herself; whether it was her career, her latest record, her problems with her management company, or the compliments her fans had tweeted, it was all about Chloe.

Finally, Edwin interrupted.

"What do you do for fun?" he asked.

"What?"

"For fun. What makes you happy?"

"Oh!" she considered. "Well, being on stage, I guess. Having people like me, and stuff."

"I mean, off stage. What does Chloe like to do?"

She made a confused, child-like face.

"I don't know. I like to have people over for parties. Like here at the Ace. I'm in the Ace Suite, and there's this terrace that can hold, like, a ton of people, so we've been having a party almost every night! It's so great!"

"So, entertaining people."

"Yeah. Oh! And I like to shop. I love buying new jewelry. Check out my latest bracelet! I just got it today."

She dangled her arm in front of his face.

"It's lovely. But what about museums?" he persist-
ed. "You've been all over the world. What are your
favorite museums in your travels?"

"Museums?" she asked, dumbfounded. She
paused as if trying to collect her thoughts. "I can't
remember the last time I was in a museum. Except
the Metropolitan Museum of Art, but I was doing a
concert for a charity thing."

"The last book you read?" he asked.

"Oh! That I can answer. It was the biography of
Michael Jackson." She seemed proud of herself.

Edwin sighed. He remembered back to his days in
drama school. One of his teachers had required the
class to bring in a current event every Monday that
had nothing to do with entertainment, to teach them
that there was more to life than their career. Than
themselves.

Edwin's mind began to drift. He was beginning
to grow weary, physically and emotionally. Adriana
needed no assignment to understand what was happening in the world around her. She was interested in
more than her own experiences.

Has it really only been one day since my birthday
party?

One day since she left.

"Edwin, you weren't listening!" Chloe whined.

"Sorry."

"I said you've got to come up and listen to some of my tracks. The ones we did in L.A. They're not finished yet, but Bradford's gonna tweak them, add some techno beats and stuff. Will you come up?"

She pouted her lips.

I shouldn't.

But Adriana's just a friend. A friend who left.

"No party tonight, girls," Chloe said to her friends as they passed their table. "I promised to let Edwin hear some of the tracks."

She grabbed his hand as they headed for the elevator.

In her hotel room, Chloe kicked off her heels.

"Look!" she said, dancing across the room. "It's a record player! With like, actual vinyl records! They're in all the suites. So cool."

She poured herself and Edwin another glass of wine from a side table, and settled herself next to him on the modern sofa.

Better not drink too much more of this. Head is beginning to spin.

As she pulled up some files on her iPad, Edwin tried to take in his surroundings. The room was ultra-modern, with tones of gray, blue and black. There was a bedroom with a large, king-sized bed. The living area, where they were, was furnished with a modern leather sofa, a large oak table, and was accented with eclectic art. There was a record player on a table and an acoustic guitar hung on the wall. He could see the over-sized terrace outside the glass doors.

He watched Chloe toying with her iPad, her brow furrowed.

She belongs in this room. Young, modern.

Beautiful.

"Here we go," Chloe said, snuggling up to him as she pushed play.

Edwin jolted as the song began. Chloe's music was obviously intended for the dance floor. Edwin hadn't been dancing in a club since university, and even then, he hadn't really enjoyed it. He went because it was expected. He typically stayed close to the bar. And the bathroom.

He drained his wine glass.

Chloe closed her eyes as she listened, a big, vacant grin across her face. When her vocals came in, Edwin winced.

"Those are just scratch vocals," Chloe explained. "I'll be doing the real tracks next week."

Edwin was relieved.

I hope it sounds better than this when they're finished.

The song ended.

"What did you think?" she asked, curling up and touching his shoulder with her fingers.

Edwin nodded. "Yes, it was—quite—"

"Thank you!" she said without waiting for him to finish. "This album's gonna be so great. It has to be, actually. If Bradford doesn't give me a hit this time, he's gone."

Edwin was surprised to see a serious tone in her voice. Yet it still sounded childish, like a little girl who didn't get her way.

She refilled his glass.

"My last album—well, it wasn't a flop, it just didn't sell as many as it should have. So I need this one to get me back on top. Can't have Amaya winning everything at the Grammys!"

With that comment, she smiled, but Edwin could see the contempt in her eyes.

Don't want to get in her way.

He took another sip of wine.

"Edwin," she crooned, taking his wine glass from his hand and setting it on the table. She nestled closer to him and pushed a button on a remote control, dimming the lights. "Thank you for coming tonight. I think we've got so much in common."

"Do you?" he asked as she ran her fingers through his curls.

She smells like sandalwood.

He smoothed her golden hair back from her face.

Chloe moved closer.

"I think we get along very well, don't you?" she asked.

"Mm-hmm."

Having things in common isn't everything.

"We're both famous. We're both rich. We're both beautiful."

"You think I'm beautiful?" he asked.

She laughed. "Handsome, then."

She moved in for a kiss.

Why not? What's wrong with kissing?

He kissed her pouty red lips.

Kissing's nice. I like kissing.

Knowing current events isn't everything.

Suddenly, despite Edwin's spinning brain, Adriana's face appeared in the place of Chloe's. He was kissing her in the Cradle Walk, and—

No. This isn't right.

He pulled back.

"Chloe—" he began to protest.

But Chloe didn't take the hint. She wrapped her arms around his neck and nearly flung herself at him.

"Oh, Edwin!" she cried.

She was kissing him all over his face, his ears, his chest. She pushed him backward on the couch and landed on top of him.

"Chloe!" he said, grabbing her hands that were working their way through the buttons on his shirt.

He forced himself to a sitting position.

"What's wrong?" she asked, pouting and sitting back.

"This is a little too much, too fast," he said. "We hardly know each other, and—"

He didn't think it wise to mention another woman's name.

"And I respect you too much."

That worked.

"Aw, how sweet!" she cooed. She twisted one of his curls around her finger.

"I think I should go," he added, attempting to stand.

"No! You don't have to do that," she said, grabbing his hand. "I know you respect me, but—"

"No, really. I should go. I'm not feeling all that well."

He ran his hand across his perspiring forehead.

"Call me tomorrow?" she asked, batting her lashes at him as she buttoned his shirt again. She hesitated, her hands on his chest.

He stepped backward.

"Yes. Tomorrow," he promised, heading for the door.

In the elevator, he pulled his hands through his hair, contemplating his narrow escape.

What was I thinking?

I wasn't thinking.

She's the last thing I need right now. I'm better off alone.

Stupid, stupid wine.

He was able to sneak past the Hoi Polloi on the ground floor where he knew Chloe's friends and fans were still congregating. But he'd forgotten about the reporters until it was too late. He stepped outside the doors of the hotel and was greeted by riotous fans screaming, flashes of light, and a hailstorm of questions.

"What's the story with you and Chloe, Edwin? Are you together?"

"Look's like you've had a steamy night already!"

Edwin pushed past them and into the cab the doorman hailed.

He collapsed in the backseat.

"Rough night, eh?" asked the cabbie.

"Yes," he answered, then noticed the cabbie's amused looks. "What do you mean?" he asked.

The cabbie pointed to his face and turned the rearview mirror so Edwin could see his own reflection.

There was red lipstick smeared across his mouth and cheeks.

Brilliant!

21

His agent was the first call in the morning.

"Is everything all right, dear?" Debra asked.

As if I'm a troubled teenager.

"Yes, Debra. Everything's fine."

He winced as he swallowed some ibuprofen for his aching head.

Too much wine.

Too much Chloe.

"Well, you're all over the gossip columns this morning. I just wanted to know if—you meant to be. Is this another one of David's stunts?" she asked, a hint of anger in her motherly voice.

"No, David had nothing to do with it," he assured her. "I don't even want to look this time."

"Lipstick smears, Edwin? It just makes you look, well, tacky."

He could feel her entire generation shudder.

"Nothing happened. Well, not nothing. But not what you think. She just wears a lot of lipstick."

"Hmmh," Debra grunted. "Now, about that script. The one about the alien invasion."

"I don't want to do it," said Edwin.

"Why?"

"It's just not—not serious enough. I want something completely different. Something substantial. Challenging."

She sighed. "Okay. I'll keep looking. But you can't turn down everything or you'll stop getting offers."

"I know," he said.

I just can't think straight right now.

Edwin did not call Chloe the next day. Or the next. In fact, he avoided her calls altogether. He finally replied to her multiple texts, claiming to be swamped with work. He was thankful she was busy working on her record because it allowed her to become self-absorbed. He felt stupid and used, but mostly stupid. And he had used Chloe. She may not have cared, but he knew it was true, and he hated himself for it.

That's not who I am.

I'm not Mary Alice Rowan.

He waited three days, however, before he attempted to call Adriana. But, like she said, he couldn't get in touch with her. Her cell phone was turned off. He couldn't even find her on Find My Friends.

Adriana unavailable.

He emailed her and got an automated response. She had no home phone, and her number at work was automated and dropped him into her voice mailbox, which said she was unavailable and to call a colleague instead. He knew she either wasn't listening to her messages, or was ignoring his.

She never called.

He had nothing to go on to find her. No address. No hotel. No scrap of information she had dropped. Nothing.

The only thing of interest came from his driver, Bill, who had slunk over to Edwin's, in fear of his job, to report a conversation he had overheard between Bethany and Adriana the night she left.

According to Bill, Adriana had cried after the argument. Bethany was not so sympathetic.

"Well," Bethany had said, "that went well. That's exactly why I told you not to tell him you were leaving."

"What did you expect me to do?" Adriana had demanded of her friend. "I couldn't lie to him. I couldn't pretend that I would see him tomorrow, and then just not be there!"

"We shouldn't have come to this party. You shouldn't be in England at all. It was a distraction."

"It was his thirty-fifth birthday! It meant a lot to him!"

"*You* mean a lot to him!" said Bethany. "And it's getting dangerous."

Bill said they ended the conversation there and were silent the rest of the drive. Edwin tucked the information in his mind, but it didn't make sense to him. Why would it be dangerous for her to mean a lot to him?

And she did mean a lot to him. He didn't realize how much until that night. Chloe had put it all out of his mind temporarily; he hadn't wanted to think about it, about what he had said to Adriana.

I love you.

What was I thinking?

I wasn't thinking.

It just blurted out on its own. And she ran away because—because I love her.

His imagination replayed the scene: Adriana getting into the car, turning her tearful face away. The nameless, faceless man loomed up again, out of the flashes of cameras, blocking his view of the car speeding away to some unknown destination. Carrying her away from him.

When he couldn't get Adriana, he turned to Bethany. Call after call went unheeded. He even marched down to the British Museum, only to be told she refused to see him due to "work". He did the only thing he knew to do: appealed to the feminine side of her predatory bird personality. He sent her a note via the guard that read: My heart is breaking.

It worked.

Bethany appeared, disheveled again, but with a slight look of sympathy.

"I don't know where she is," she said.

"I don't believe you," he replied.

She shrugged. "Nevertheless, I don't know where she is." She folded her arms and stared at him.

"Can you give her a message for me?" he asked.

"I told you, I don't—"

"For when you see her again. Or hear from her. Or something."

She appeared to relent, shifting her weight to the other foot.

"Just tell her—tell her I'm sorry. Tell her I want to be a good friend."

She nodded. "If I hear from her, I'll tell her."

She returned to the archives, the great door closing solemnly and finally behind her.

Edwin knew that was all he would glean from the Museum.

22

The next series of *Dr. Hanover* episodes looked promising to Edwin. He was looking forward to the action scenes, and he always enjoyed the rapid and witty dialogue between the characters. It was something he had to prepare for; it required a great deal of concentration and focus. He hoped he was up to the challenge this year. He had never had the kind of distractions he was dealing with. He had never had a mystery woman before.

He was actually thankful for the hectic schedule that being back on set would bring, knowing it would help him get his mind on other things. But it also meant people. And Edwin was tired of people. He especially hated the looks they gave him. His personal life was so on display now, he felt like he was starring in his own reality show.

Jen came to the set with him everyday. Her constant looks of motherly concern, despite the fact that she was about ten years his junior, caused him to be moody and snappy around her.

None of her business.

His makeup artist on the set gave him looks of pity. Poor Edwin. If he just loved me instead.

Get a boyfriend.

Crew members looked at him smugly, as if to say, 'You're not as great as you thought, mate.'

Try living my life.

Harry flat out told him Adriana was out of his league, anyway, and to stick with models, like he does.

"It's the thinking girls who cause you trouble, Ed," Harry had said, with all of the wisdom he had accrued in his 26 years of life. "Stick with Chloe."

Genevieve was the most helpful, if only because she was so matter-of-fact.

"I missed the domestic at the party," she had said the first day back on set. "I was busy with my own domestic. John called Pierre Ferrar a Frenchie, and that didn't go over so well with Pierre, although he really is a Frenchie. I thought he was going to hit John in the face with the duck paté, which really would have been a shame. It was an excellent duck paté. Anyway, darling, I truly am sorry. But you're supposed to be in love with *me*. Everyone knows you're supposed to fall in love with your love interest on the show."

"I *do* love you, Genevieve," Edwin had said.

"Of course you do, darling, but that doesn't count. You're not *in* love with me. If you would just fall in love with me, all this Mystery Woman and Chloe drama would go away. It's only proper."

Edwin smiled and kissed her hand.

"Thank you, Genevieve. I'll try."

He knew this was Genevieve's way of saying she was sorry for his troubles, but she wouldn't bring it up again. And he appreciated it.

Life on the set was always oscillating from complete chaos to complete boredom. Edwin always felt that the waiting took more out of him than the action. Waiting for lighting, waiting for sound equipment to work properly, waiting for script rewrites at the last minute. And this time, he didn't want time on his hands. He didn't want to think about what she was doing or when he would see her again.

He had become an avid news watcher in the past few weeks. He convinced himself that it was only to pass the time. Like the internet research he was doing on oil in the Middle East. And Ahmet Tastan in particular. It was how he learned that Mr. Tastan was back in Turkey, but was continuing with his initiative to make deals with Europe and America. Edwin wondered if he himself would be as dedicated to something, if he could feel so strongly about something that he would be willing to risk his life. Edwin was sure Mr. Tastan's life was still in danger.

"Petrol prices are so high right now," complained

Genevieve after her commute to the studio one morning. Genevieve was known for her love of cars and driving. "It costs almost as much to fill my tank as it does to color my hair. Not that I'm not a natural blonde, of course."

"That's why I have the studio pick me up," commented Harry with a smirk.

"Well, it's because oil companies won't budge on their prices," Edwin explained. "They want a high price per barrel, even though oil production is high. I mean, so many people are moving toward more efficient vehicles, so petrol isn't as much in demand. There's a glut, so to speak. Which is why we should be seeing a reduction in prices—with demand being lower—but instead, the oil companies are wanting to keep their profit. Which is why a company like Kara Inci is so helpful to the common consumer. They want to sell at a lower price, banking on more oil being sold because it's more affordable."

Harry and Genevieve stared at him. Harry's mouth was hanging open, making him resemble a codfish. Genevieve blinked her long, fake lashes a few times.

"Well," she said finally, "I, for one, would never consider myself a 'common consumer'."

One side of her mouth curved up in a mischievous smile.

"Of course not, Genevieve," agreed Edwin quickly. "There's nothing common about you."

He gave her a charming smile in return as he rose and headed for the bathroom.

I should stop reading *World Oil*.

23

It was two weeks to the day since she left, and still no word from Adriana. Gossip blogs had grown bored and moved on. Even the photos of him with smears of red lipstick had faded.

Short attention span.

It was a rare day. Edwin was not expected on set until evening. He decided to go out for a walk around the city. Despite his hatred of exercise, walking was always the one activity that calmed his mind and lifted his spirits.

The sun was shining, but it wasn't enough to ward off the chill. Autumn was definitely making its appearance. Leaves were changing colors and the days were shorter.

Although he told himself he had no particular place to go, he quickly found himself in Kensington.

Might as well walk along the Broad Walk. It's always beautiful this time of year.

The smaller of the trees, he noticed, had already changed to bright orange and russet, but many of the tallest ones still held onto their green hue, as if they were unable to make up their mind what season they were in. Edwin noticed quite a few mothers with children playing in the grass or making leaf piles, and the occasional dog-walker stumbled by with a handful of leashes.

It turned out to be a colder day than Edwin expected. He walked briskly to warm himself and soon found himself in front of the white statue of Queen Victoria. He felt like she was judging him from her exalted position, as if she disagreed with how he handled his last moments with Adriana.

Can't get her out of my mind.

Kensington certainly wasn't the place to forget her. He set his jaw as he approached the Palace and the familiar places they had walked.

There was the Sunken Garden. There was the Cradle Walk. Many of the leaves had turned yellow on the lime trees, which showed brightly against the crimson stems. When he came to it, he found he couldn't go in. He lowered his head into the cold, autumn wind and walked on.

Within minutes, he had arrived at the Orangery. Edwin's plaid cap and wool scarf were no match for the biting air. He decided a cup of tea would be a good idea before heading home.

As he stepped through the French doors, he was instantly recognized by the Polish maitre'd.

"*Mr. Sterling*! So happy to greet you again!"

He looked around and behind Edwin.

"No beautiful lady friend?" he asked. "No Bruce Lee impersonator?"

"Not this time," Edwin replied.

Maybe this was a mistake, coming here.

The maitre'd showed him to a table, then paused for a moment.

"I hope you don't think me im*per*tinent," he began, "but I *must* tell you, I would stay away from the *blonde*, if I was you. I've heard—things!"

"Chloe? What kind of things?" asked Edwin, intrigued.

"Well, I don't like to *gossip*, but my friend Christine works for the hotel where she's staying, and she says she's rude, rude, rude. Orders people around, even her own friends. A woman like that—" He shook his head. "She's what's called 'high-maintenance'."

Edwin nodded.

My thoughts exactly.

The meal was uneventful. The maitre'd busied himself with other patrons, and the waiter did not seem to have been there on that fateful summer day to witness Adriana's self-defense extravaganza; he didn't ask any awkward questions.

Edwin left the Orangery refreshed, and stood for a moment on the short flight of steps that led to the avenue of holly trees. He had stood there that day, too, waiting for Adriana. The holly trees were unchanged, of course, being evergreens, except for the abundance of bright red berries that now adorned them. The squirrels were nowhere to be seen, but the birds were out in numbers, eating their way toward winter.

His mind went back to that day, so long ago it seemed now. How happy he had been, touring the palace with Adriana by his side. Then the strange request to remain friends. Then the crazy fan and Adriana's remarkable ability to disarm her. Trained, she said, by watching her brother's karate class.

A brilliant idea went through Edwin's mind. She has a brother! Maybe she went to visit him! Surely that is obtainable information. And what about her father? She said her mother was dead, but what if her father isn't? Hope surged through him for a moment. Then, just as quickly, it faded.

Why do I even care? I must train myself not to care.

He began the walk through the holly avenue. He was lost in his own thoughts, and didn't see or hear the group of young women who laughingly poured out of Kensington Palace as he passed.

"Edwin!"

He looked up at the sound of his name.

It was Chloe.

Their eyes met. Edwin braced himself for the on-slaught of her wrath. After a few meager texts, he had stopped contacting her altogether. She had left a few voicemails afterward; the last one was tearful, asking him if he even cared for her at all.

He didn't, so he hadn't called back.

Now here she was, at Kensington, probably doing one of her historical tours to get inspiration for her album.

After a few brief seconds of hesitation, she nearly ran to him, a huge smile engulfing her face. She embraced him, giving him a peck on each cheek. Edwin was so surprised, he forgot to cringe.

She was wearing a bright red cape with a hood that matched the stain of her lips. She looked like Little Red Riding Hood.

Or the wolf in disguise.

"Edwin, you naughty boy!" she teased. "I haven't seen you in all this time! I'm nearly finished with my album!"

She playfully slapped him on the chest. Then she reached up and rubbed the lipstick marks off his cheeks.

"Wouldn't want a repeat of those naughty photo-graphs!" she teased.

Her friends tittered. Edwin recognized Marianne and Shelly from the Hoi Polloi. They had another friend with them with a camera; her job was clearly to document Chloe's time in London. She took several snaps of the two of them together, including one of Chloe rubbing the lipstick off his cheek.

Irritating. She's definitely going to milk this.

"What are you doing here? *We* were touring the Palace. It's so awesome! And so historical."

Now Edwin did cringe.

"I was just out for a walk," he explained.

"You know," she said, taking his arm, "I was *just* thinking I'd like to take a walk today."

There was a chorus of giggles from her retinue.

"I'll join you!" she said, as if giving him a present.

The last thing Edwin wanted was to take a walk with Chloe, but he felt guilty for using her to get back at Adriana, and her surprising goodwill toward him caught him off guard. What would David advise?

No scenes in public.

"My friends were just going back to the hotel. *Weren't* you, girls? I know you all need to rest."

There was disappointed agreement from the group. The girl with the camera hesitated.

"Shoo!" said Chloe, waving her on. The ladies quickly took their leave of him and headed across the park.

Two dark-suited men with earpieces stayed, however, and followed a few paces behind Chloe. Edwin hadn't noticed them before.

Bodyguards, I guess.

Edwin wondered if the bodyguards were necessary, or an accessory, like the bracelets spiraling down her arm.

Chloe chattered away. The album was going well, according to her, and her record label was excited about its future release. Edwin found it easy to contemplate his own thoughts because she only needed a nod here or there, or an assentive, "Hmm. That's amazing."

Thoughts of the last visit to Kensington caused him to think of Mr. Tastan. He envisioned him relaxing in his cushy flat, feeling safe, oblivious to the fact that someone wanted to blow him up. A second attempt on his life in just a few days. Who wanted him dead, and why? And the question that Edwin thought was the most intriguing: why had they failed twice?

He led Chloe down the Broad Walk toward Kensington Road. It couldn't be said that the two celebrities did not attract attention as they strolled under the brightly-colored trees. The red cape and hood alone was enough to turn heads. But the bodyguards dissuaded any autograph-seekers.

At last they were in front of the building he had been looking for. It was a Georgian, painted white, with black, iron lettering that read "The Swan". Each flat was really one of a series of row houses, each with its own door. There was a brass plaque on one of the doors that announced it was the office.

"I need to go in here for a minute," he said to Chloe.

"Oh." She stopped her flow of chattering long enough to look around her.

"Where are we?" she asked, frowning.

Edwin pushed open the door, and stopped. Someone was sitting in a chair, talking with a woman who appeared to be the Office Manager. Edwin recognized the back of the head immediately.

24

"Phillip?" he said, incredulously.

Phillip turned.

"Edwin!"

The two men stared at each other. Phillip stood.

"And...Chloe," he added, surprised, glancing at the two bodyguards who bookended the door.

"We were taking a walk," explained Edwin.

Awkward.

"I see."

"What are you doing here, Phillip?" asked Edwin.

"Same as you, I think," he said in a low voice. "Seeing where it happened."

"Or didn't happen," said Edwin.

"Oh my goodness!" exclaimed the well-dressed woman at the desk, adjusting her glasses. "Are you Chloe?"

Chloe smiled a dazzling smile, eager to please a fan.

"And Edwin Sterling?" she said, shifting her gaze. "Are you looking for a flat to rent?"

She seemed gleefully hopeful.

"Sorry, no. I just, um..." Edwin stuttered.

Should have thought this out more.

"Miss Black was assuring me that our friend, the Count, has nothing to worry about if he rents one of her flats," said Phillip, coming to the rescue. "She was just telling me about *that day*."

"Yes," said Miss Black. "I was just telling Mr. Kingsley-March that the bomb was found in a gift basket. I remember it had a tin of Turkish tea in it, because I wondered if Turkish tea would be as good as British tea, and it had food and other goodies in it. And a bomb."

Chloe clutched her throat dramatically.

"A bomb?" she squealed.

"In the tea canister, of all things! I guess it's a good thing I didn't try some!" Miss Black tittered. "But seriously, it was fortunate that the bomb squad arrived before anyone was hurt."

The two men agreed.

"Although I'm not sure who called," she said, puzzled. "They just showed up."

Chloe looked dumbfounded, her scarlet mouth hanging open slightly.

"They didn't mention that in the papers," said Phillip to Edwin. "About the bomb being in a gift basket."

"Oh, Mr. Sterling," said Miss Black, "it's interesting that you're here because I saw your lady friend that morning. I meant to mention it to someone at the time, but it was quite chaotic, as you can imagine." She smiled at him, like someone giving good news.

"My lady friend?" he asked.

Chloe's head snapped in his direction.

"Your Mystery Woman."

Adriana?

"You saw her here?" asked Phillip, exchanging glances with Edwin.

She's not a killer, Edwin thought defiantly.

"Yes. She was here. I remember because I had just seen the photographs of you both at the Bella Luna. I sometimes check the *Gossip Gazette* online, and I had thought, how cute! It's good for him to have a girlfriend. And then, here she was. Well, not here, exactly. The building where it happened is two doors down. They rented the entire three floors. Had all kinds of important-looking people in and out."

"And she was in the building?" asked Edwin.

"Well, when I saw her, she had just come out of the building. Now, come to think of it, I wonder what she was doing there? I didn't think about it at the time. I was just so excited to recognize her. I was looking around for you, but you weren't with her. Maybe she knew Mr. Tastan."

The Office Manager didn't seem particularly concerned. It was as if bombs being planted in her building were commonplace.

Shards of memory flashed through Edwin's brain. Adriana waiting at the Palace Gate, her cheeks pink. Slightly out-of-breath. Had she been running?

"That must have been it," Phillip said, nodding to Miss Black. "Well, thank you for your time."

"Sure," said Miss Black. "You can tell your friend, Count Cristo, that there's no danger. He'll be safe with us. We are extra careful about all of our deliveries now, that's for sure."

Outside on the sidewalk, Edwin cornered his friend.

"Count Cristo?" he asked.

"Why, yes. You remember our friend the Count. Monty Cristo. He's thinking of taking one of these flats for a week, but was concerned about the bomb threat."

"The Count of Monte Cristo?" asked Edwin, his blue eyes twinkling.

Phillip shrugged. "Apparently, Miss Black doesn't read."

"You know a Count?" asked Chloe.

25

The three headed down Kensington Road toward Royal Albert Hall.

"So," began Phillip. "Any news?"

Edwin shook his head. "Not a word."

"Are you talking about that girl from the birthday party?" asked Chloe, pouting, her penciled brows furrowed.

Edwin ignored her. "I had an idea, though," he said to Phillip. "She has a brother, and a father. I wonder if I can get information on them? She may be there, with her family."

Phillip looked up sheepishly. "I may have some information on that."

"What do you mean?"

"Well," he said, apologetically, "You know Jeff works in the Home Office now."

"Yes." Cyril Jefferson was an old schoolmate of Phillip's and Edwin's.

"I asked Jeff to look into it for me. Do a background check, so to speak. It was actually right after she left England the first time. Before your birthday party."

Edwin glared at Phillip.

Why doesn't he trust my judgement?

"Do you want to know what he found, or not?" continued Phillip.

"Fine."

"He says she does have a brother. He's in the Marines, but he's on some secret mission somewhere and can't be reached right now. Apparently, he did take karate. Won some championships."

"I think karate is so cool," commented Chloe. "Those karate guys can do so many tricks. I should take karate. I'm going to tell my manager when I get back to the hotel."

Phillip exchanged an irritated look with Edwin.

"Her mother was of Turkish descent, from a wealthy family who left the country after World War I. Her father was an American businessman. Something to do with shipping oil."

"Was?" Edwin asked.

"Both parents are dead. Died in a small plane accident about five years ago."

Edwin's shoulders dropped. "So, a dead end," he sighed.

"Afraid so."

They walked in silence. Phillip had the somber expression of a doctor who has just given a fatal prognosis. Edwin stuffed his hands in his pockets. His obvious disappointment quickly turned to anger and self-pity.

It doesn't matter. She doesn't matter.

Police cars in front of The Swan. People gathered. That couple in the Orangery who couldn't get through. And Adriana was there, all the time. At the Palace Gate, pretending to be oblivious to what was going on behind her. Sitting at the Orangery, passively listening to the American couple complain. Suddenly, her polite smile turned into a mocking sneer. "And I almost got away with it!"

No. Edwin pushed the thoughts out of his mind.

Whatever she is, she can't be a killer.

"What's that?" asked Chloe suddenly, pointing with admiration at a large, extremely ornate, golden monument.

"That's the Albert Memorial," explained Phillip. "To honor Queen Victoria's husband, Prince Albert."

"That's what I need," she said. The two men looked questioningly at her.

Chloe was staring up at the monument, a dreamy, far-away expression in her wide blue eyes.

"I need a statue like that. Of me, of course."

Edwin started to laugh, but stopped short.

She's not joking.

She continued making plans in her own mind.

"It would be golden like that, with all kinds of

carving on it. I could use it as part of my stage set. Oh my gosh! Wouldn't it be great?"

She clutched Edwin's arm ecstatically.

"I could have the dancers carry it out. No! I've got it! I'll paint myself gold and be the statue myself!"

Edwin exchanged wide-eyed looks with Phillip, who covered his mouth with his hand to stifle a smile.

"Oh, Edwin! This is going to be the most spectacular show idea yet! I'll come out as the statue on a throne, and the dancers can carry me out and then I'll come down the steps and sing "Queen of Everything"!" She wrapped her arms around herself and grinned at the Albert Memorial.

"Thank you, Edwin!" she said rapturously.

"For what?" he asked.

"For bringing me by this...whose memorial did you say it was?"

"Prince Albert. You know, husband of Victoria? You would have learned about him at Kensington today."

"Oh yeah. Didn't he die or something? And then she only wore black." She shuddered. "Such a horrible fashion statement. And she got literally fat!"

"She was in mourning," Phillip said quietly, trying not to be offended.

"The whole fashion community was in mourning,"

she said. "But I'll be golden and skinny. Don't you think I'll be beautiful, all golden and stuff?" She batted her eyes at Edwin.

Looking back, Edwin couldn't decide whether it was her narcissism, her complete disregard for a mourning Queen, or simply that he was angry about Adriana, but instead of making a benign compliment in return, Edwin said:

"I think you'll look ridiculous."

Watching her face blanche white made him secretly pleased, even though he knew it could backfire on him.

"What?" she demanded. He could see the rage behind her eyes.

Interesting. So near the surface.

"I think making yourself into a golden statue would be narcissistic and arrogant and shows how out of touch with reality you are."

"Slow down, mate," warned Phillip, placing a hand on his shoulder.

"I have never been so offended in my life!" Chloe shouted. Her bodyguards moved in closer. "I've been a superstar since I was sixteen-years-old because I've always had great ideas! Everyone says so! I even write my own songs! Most of the time!"

"Of course everyone says you're great! Because if they didn't, they'd be fired!"

Chloe screamed with rage, stamping her feet on the sidewalk. "I'm going back to my hotel! And I am going to be a golden statue, and I'm not going to be your friend!"

She pushed her way through Edwin and Phillip, tossing her golden hair, her red hood bobbing behind her. The bodyguards marched after her. One began hailing a cab.

"You're a horrible man, Edwin Sterling!" she shouted over her shoulder as she waited on the corner for her cab. "I don't blame that other girl one bit for refusing to talk to you anymore!"

As he watched, jealousy rose up in her. It was more important for her to be 'Edwin Sterling's girl-friend' than it was for her to save face.

"But if you want to be my friend again, Edwin Sterling," she sneered, pointing a shaking finger at him, "you're going to have to apologize!"

She folded her arms and glared at him, waiting for him to do so. He didn't.

Instead, he gestured a salute at her and began walking the other way. Phillip followed.

"I'm at the Ace Hotel!" she called after him.

Neither man said a word until they had put some distance between themselves and the golden statue.

"How old is Chloe?" Edwin asked Phillip after a time.

"I don't know. Twenty-four?"

Edwin nodded. "I don't think she matured past the glorious age of sixteen," he observed. He couldn't keep himself from grinning. They both started laughing. Edwin wiped tears from his eyes.

"I can't believe you said that to her," Phillip said, still chuckling.

"I don't know what came over me. But, I guess I can't be her friend anymore," he said with mocked sadness.

"Unless you apologize!" said Phillip in his best Chloe voice. "She's at the Ace Hotel!"

They laughed some more.

"What a day this has been. Full of surprises," Edwin said.

"You're telling me," said his friend.

Edwin took a more serious tone. "Thanks for trying to find out about Adriana's family, even though I suspect you were looking for dirt on her."

"I love a good mystery, same as you, Dr. Hanover," Phillip explained. "Adriana's disappearance has me just as puzzled. I wish I could find her for you. It's odd, though, her being at The Swan the day of the bombing."

I don't want to talk about it.

"Do you think she knows him?" Phillip mused. "She was in both places at the time of—"

"What are you suggesting?" Edwin snapped.

"I don't know. Calm down."

Phillip glanced around him.

"Lower your voice, Edwin. This is serious stuff."

"She's not a killer, Phillip. I won't believe it."

Phillip wasn't quick to agree.

"Well," he said finally, "she obviously wasn't the attempted shooter at the Museum. He's dead."

"So she's a bomber?"

"Why was she there?" Phillip demanded.

"I don't know. Maybe she did know him and came for a visit," Edwin suggested.

"And then failed to mention it to you when it's all over the news."

Edwin shook his head.

He remembered the sound of her voice over the phone. "Why should I care about Mr. Tastan?"

"I won't believe that she's a murderer, Phillip. There's got to be another explanation."

Phillip stopped walking and faced his friend.

"I do want you to be happy, Edwin," he insisted. "I don't want her to be involved in this. I hope she's not. And I'm sorry I couldn't be more helpful in finding her family or something."

Edwin nodded.

"Sometimes I wish I actually was Dr. Hanover," he joked grimly. "Then I'd be able to make sense of all of this."

"We need better writers," Phillip agreed.

26

Filming was over for *Dr. Hanover*. Normally, Edwin would celebrate the break in his schedule by going on holiday with friends. This year, he didn't feel like celebrating, and he didn't want to be with people and their frivolous, happy, annoying lives. He also wasn't sure he could outrun the paparazzi, no matter where he went.

Instead, he was still in his robe in the middle of the afternoon, drinking coffee and staring at his phone. As he checked the news, an entertainment article caught his eye, and he tortured himself once again by reading about himself and Chloe. The past few weeks had been tabloid hell. Chloe's photographer friend had twittered her photos of the two of them looking friendly in Kensington Gardens, with comments that suggested they were dating. The tabloid websites had taken the bait.

"*Two Women in Two Weeks*? Edwin Sterling's Steamy Love Life."

One article claiming to have inside knowledge actually suggested that Edwin and Chloe should be amalgamated into ChloEd.

Media opinion had turned quickly, however. To add fodder to those who accused him of being an angry and ill-tempered lover, some unknown iPhone user had recorded the fight in front of the Prince Albert Memorial. The internet went crazy, suggesting the reason for his continued singleness was his inability to get along well with others.

David's words still haunted him.

Worst. Move. Yet. You'll probably end up in a song.

I'll probably end up in a song trying to get you out of this.

Edwin clicked off of news and onto another favorite app.

Find My Friends.

Although he hated to admit it, Edwin had checked the app every day since the day she left, and every day, it had the same response.

Adriana unavailable.

It can't be stalking if she's unavailable.

It had now been nearly five weeks since he had last seen or heard from her. He thought it would get easier with time. But not even the newfound knowledge of her presence at The Swan had caused him to write her off for good. Much to his aggravation, he found himself thinking about her, wondering about her, worrying about her.

At one point he had remembered the photograph he had saved to his desktop, the one of him and Adriana in front of the Bella Luna. In moments of weakness, he would gaze at it, thinking of her, remembering their time together. The photographer had captured the moment when she had looked up at him, pure happiness in her eyes.

Why did she run from it?

Will she ever run back?

Sometimes she came to him in dreams, but they were more like nightmares. In one recurring dream, she stood on his doorstep with a gift basket.

"Would you like some tea, Edwin?" she would ask, smiling her intoxicating smile.

When he tried to close the door, she would suddenly develop Amazonian strength; he couldn't get the door closed, no matter how hard he tried.

He always woke up in a cold sweat.

She's not a killer.

His mother called, interrupting his revery.

"Edwin. What are you doing?"

"I'm just sitting at home."

"You know what I mean. I keep reading things about you on the internet."

"Mother, I haven't done anything wrong."

"Why do they think you're dating that Red Riding Hood character?"

"I don't know."

"Yes, you do. Now listen to me. Your father and I agree. You just need to be patient and wait for her."

"It's been five weeks, Mother. It's over. She's not coming back."

"She will."

"You can't know that."

"Yes, I can. Because your father asked her to. At your birthday party. Before you made her angry and she ran away."

"Oh my God."

"You'll see, my dear. She's trustworthy."

He hung up the phone.

Trustworthy.

My parents seem to have the script of my life. I guess my copy's lost.

Debra called him with an offer for a new film.

"It's a psychological thriller, and you'd be the murderer," she explained, as if he'd be pleased.

Great.

"I know you're going through some things, Edwin, but I really need you to give this one a read. It could be your next hit."

The last thing Edwin wanted to think about was another hit, another reason to be in the news or on the internet. But maybe playing the killer would be to his advantage. He already felt like he destroyed everything he touched.

The doorbell rang, startling him.

Paparazzi again?

He hesitated even going to the door, until he recognized the knock.

It was Phillip.

Edwin let him in, suspiciously eyeing a newspaper he had tucked under his arm.

More tabloid headlines. What now.

"Shouldn't you be at work?" Edwin asked.

"Yes, but this is important. I had to come immediately. You know how you've been somewhat in the news of late?" Phillip asked. "Well, so has someone else."

He handed Edwin the paper. It was folded to a picture of a man and a woman at a restaurant. Above the photograph was the familiar headline.

"*Who is the Mystery Woman?*"

Edwin rolled his eyes. What do they have on me now?

He scrutinized the photo. It was not a photograph of him. A young man, seemingly of Middle Eastern descent, was leaning close to a woman, speaking into her ear. She was turned away from him slightly, looking down. But she was unmistakeable.

"Adriana!"

Edwin looked up at Phillip with a mixture of thankfulness and pain.

Adriana found. But Adriana with someone else?

Someone else's Mystery Woman.

"I was passing a news stand, and I saw that headline. Naturally, I thought it was about you. Sorry. But when I saw the picture, I knew it was her. So I bought it, because it says where they are."

Phillip pointed to the bottom of the photograph.

Edwin read the caption.

"Who is the mystery woman with Bahranian playboy, Hazzim Nejem? Hazzim was seen with this beautiful brunette while on holiday at Istanbul's Ciragan Palace Hotel. Will she be the one to snag this famous bachelor?"

Istanbul. Turkey.

"What are you going to do?" asked Phillip.

I'm going to be sick.

27

The next morning, Edwin found himself on a flight to Istanbul.

He rubbed his face with his hands, trying to slow his racing mind. He had barely slept the night before. His head throbbed in pain.

Forgot to eat breakfast.

Forgot to eat dinner.

He was thankful when the stewardess handed him a meal tray.

Get yourself together. Focus on why you're doing this.

Why am I doing this?

The hours after the discovery of the photograph were primarily a blur. He could remember fragments: picking up the phone to ask a surprised Jen to make travel arrangements; Phillip questioning him.

"Are you sure you want to get involved in this, Edwin?" Phillip had asked with great concern. "She's with another man. It's what we've been saying all along."

"It's what *you've* been saying," was his spiteful reply.

Jen calling back to give him his arrangements. "I was able to find out Hazzim Nejem is staying in the Sultan's Suite. I pretended you were a friend, and they told me. So I booked you in one of the nearby suites. Edwin?"

"What?" he had growled.

"Are you sure—?"

"Of course I'm sure!"

Hours staring at the photograph. She's turned away from him. She doesn't want his attention. I know it.

If he knew nothing else, he knew he had to go to her, if only to find out the truth in person. To face her. No more secrets.

No more standing by the refreshments table.

Istanbul in October was twenty degrees warmer than the London he left behind. Edwin took off his warm coat when he stepped outside and into the waiting car service sent by the hotel.

It was his first time in the city, and he was surprised to find it such a mix of old and new.

Like London, I suppose. Ancient sites beside modern buildings.

History and future.

They passed bazaars and street vendors selling their wares. Flowers were still abundant, spilling out of windows and filling the parks he passed. The traffic was noisy and seemingly endless; Edwin felt like each car was an ant after someone disturbs the mound: directionless, yet aggressive.

It was almost an hour's drive from the airport to the hotel. Edwin closed his eyes. He forced himself to remember the details he had learned about his rival.

Once he had realized Edwin couldn't be persuaded out of going to Istanbul, Phillip had searched the internet for information on Hazzim Nejem.

"He's the heir to BOC, the Bahrain Oil Company," Phillip had told him. "He's a billionaire, or will be. Spends money like it's water, apparently, but lacks his father's work ethic. Went to Cambridge. From what I can see, he's always on holiday. There's a lot of pictures of him in fancy places with fancy people."

Phillip had shoved the laptop in Edwin's direction. There were dozens of photographs of the young man: at the beach, on a yacht, entering or leaving night clubs in ritzy neighborhoods. In all of them, he had a beautiful woman on his arm, sometimes stars he recognized. Edwin had shoved it back to Phillip in disgust.

Gold chains.

Phillip further found he had never been married and was considered Bahrain's most eligible bachelor.

"He's Muslim," Phillip said, "but the kind most Muslims would normally disown.   Except that he's mega-wealthy. He sounds like he's just your average spoiled party boy. Loose morals and a large wallet. Buys everything he wants."

What bothered Edwin more than Adriana being attracted to a morally depraved Bahrainian playboy was what Phillip had suggested afterward.

"What if she's just a gold-digger?"

"And I don't have enough gold?" he had asked.

"Well, you aren't the heir to a billion-dollar oil company. Maybe she was impressed with herself for catching the interest of Dr. Hanover, but when it came down to it—"

I'm not enough.

The Ciragan Palace Hotel was located on the European side of the Bosphorus, the wide river that wove its way through the city, separating West from East, Europe from Asia. It was originally a 19th century palace from the Ottoman Empire, but was now a five-star hotel. Jen had told him Hazzim was staying in the Sultan's Suite, the most expensive rooms in the oldest part of the hotel, the original Sultan's Palace. There were only 11 suites of rooms in that historic section, each with a view of the Bosphorus and a 24-hour butler. Edwin was booked into one of the other suites. He wasn't sure Adriana was staying at the hotel. It was a guess. But if she wasn't, he knew she must be close by, and he hoped Hazzim would lead him to her.

His arrival at the hotel did not cause a stir, except from the hotel staff, who were used to greeting high-profile guests. *Dr. Hanover*, Edwin guessed, was not well-known in Istanbul.

As the driver deposited his luggage on the pavement and a thin young bellhop in an immaculate uniform whisked it away, Edwin stared up at the white marble building in front of him. He took a deep breath and mentally calmed himself, like he often did before filming a scene.

Play your part, Edwin.

The lobby was breathtaking. It was primarily marble, with lovely arches and columns. In the center was an Atrium, where curving staircases ascended to the floors above. Bowls of heavily-scented flowers graced tables and pedestals, and small palms and potted ficus trees brought the garden indoors. Edwin thought he would enjoy staying at the Ciragan, if it weren't for Hazzim.

"Meester Sterling!"

A short, round Turkish man approached him. He was dressed impeccably in a dark suit, with black, shiny shoes. His white hair was swooped to the side with pomade, and his full, white mustache was neatly trimmed. He boisterously shook Edwin's hand.

"I am Meester Talki, the Manager here of the Ciragan Palace Hotel. I hope you will have a splendid holiday!"

"Thank you, Mr.—"

"Talki. You are welcome, sir. May I show you to your suite, sir?"

As he was being ushered through the grand Atrium to an elevator, Edwin was surprised to hear his name called.

"Edwin Sterling?" said a bewildered male voice.

Edwin turned his head. He quickly froze his face into what he hoped was a pleasant, but innocuous expression. It was Hazzim himself.

The handsome young man strode quickly across the lobby. Edwin scanned the handful of friends he had with him, but saw only males. No Adriana.

"I thought it was you!" said Hazzim, smiling genially.

Edwin shook his outstretched hand, giving him a mild, quizzical look.

As if I've never seen him before.

As if I've never wanted to choke him.

"Ah, Meester Nejem!" said Mr. Talki, grinning and nodding.

"Hazzim Nejem," said Hazzim. "I'm a big fan

of your films! And *Dr. Hanover*! Man, that's such a great show!"

Edwin murmured the correct responses and appropriate appreciation.

"Meester Nejem is a very good guest. A very generous guest," said Mr. Talki.

"Listen," Hazzim continued, ignoring the older man. "I'm having a dinner party tonight in my suite. I'd love it if you'd join me."

"Always the best for Mr. Nejem," murmured Mr. Talki, smiling.

Hazzim had patted the lapel of Edwin's suit jacket as he spoke, as if they were old friends. It was easy to see why people were drawn to him.

"Just a few friends," Hazzim said, still smiling. "And a few lady friends." His eyebrows arched upwards. He gave Edwin a congenial slap on the shoulder. "Come! Join us! You, too, Mr. Talki. Eight o'clock."

Edwin saw his opportunity to enter his enemy's territory, and he accepted the invitation.

Dinner with Stephen Quinn.

A few lady friends. And Adriana, I hope.

28

He decided to wear his blue suit with a buttoned shirt. No tie.

I look good in this suit. So the fans say.

He stood just outside the exotic wooden doors of the Sultan's Suite, trying to gather up the courage to knock. He had rehearsed in his own mind what he would say when he saw her. What he would do. He imagined himself cool and aloof, putting the Adriana in his mind on the defensive. He imagined himself passionate and bold, sweeping her off her feet, putting the Hazzim in his mind on the defensive. He imagined himself stumbling over his words and sputtering about his feelings and acting like a complete idiot while she and Hazzim glared down their noses at him.

Maybe I shouldn't go in.

The doors swung open suddenly, revealing a uniformed butler, who bowed slightly.

Too late now.

Edwin gave him his name. The butler stepped aside, allowing him to enter the marble entryway.

Edwin's own room was magnificently decorated and luxurious in every way, but the Sultan's Suite surpassed it. Glossy parquet floors were covered with thick Turkish carpets. Crystal chandeliers hung far overhead from tall painted ceilings, illuminating the richly appointed furniture. A curving staircase led to the bedrooms on the upper floor. The rooms were decorated in a mix of West and East, a true representation of the city itself. Through the floor-to-ceiling windows, Edwin could see the lights of Istanbul reflecting on the Bosphorus as the sun was setting behind the distant hills.

Several guests had arrived before Edwin; several of the gentlemen Edwin remembered from the lobby as Hazzim's personal retinue. The others in the room were an English couple Edwin recognized as the owner of a high-profile computer software company and his wife, and several very pretty Turkish girls whom he guessed were probably high-priced call girls. They were focusing their attention on the Bahrainian young men Hazzim had brought with him.

Strange company for Adriana.

Hazzim was standing in the corner near the windows, talking on the phone in serious, quiet tones, but he raised his eyebrows in greeting to Edwin. On the other side of the room was a couple Edwin guessed to be Greek. Adriana was nowhere to be seen.

All of this for nothing.

The silent butler brought Edwin a drink in an ornately-decorated blue glass. He took it and wandered toward the English couple, who immediately recognized him and introduced themselves. Apparently Hazzim was a stockholder in the software company and had invited them to visit while he was on his extended vacation in Istanbul.

"I just met him today," explained Edwin. "Has he been here at the hotel long?"

"Weeks," said the Englishman. "That's how he always parties. Stays in one place. Always the best rooms, best food. Likes the nightlife. Occasionally he explores the area. I hear he has plans to go visit Troy in the next few days. Wanted us to go, but we're leaving tomorrow. I'm not surprised he invited you up here. He likes to meet new people. The kind of guy who always needs an audience. But he pays well for it."

There was movement again at the door. Someone was coming in. Edwin could hear the exuberant voice of Mr. Talki.

"We have a new guest in the hotel, Eleni," he was explaining to someone. "Meester Nejem invited him to dinner. A very nice young man. Quite famous. A famous actor from England."

Edwin turned when he heard himself described.

The young woman Mr. Talki was speaking to was fortunately not looking at Edwin when he first saw her, giving him time to compose himself. She was staring at Mr. Talki with wide, hazel eyes, and the color had run out of her cheeks as he had spoken.

Adriana.

She was wearing a red cocktail dress that showed off her lovely legs and gathered in a rose on one shoulder. Her long, dark hair shone in the light of the chandeliers.

Her eyes searched the room until she found him.

Fear again. Briefly, just a flicker. But there.

"Eleni!" cried Mr. Talki with concern. "Are you quite all right? You look like you have just seen a ghost!"

She smiled then, and tried to shake off her initial shock. "I'm fine," she said to the older gentleman. "I was just surprised. I know the man you speak of."

The sound of her voice was like music to Edwin's ears: familiar, beautiful, haunting.

"Edwin!" She came toward him, hands outstretched.

Everything he had planned, every word he had practiced dissolved at the sight of her. She took both his hands in a guise of intimacy, but in reality it was a way of keeping him at a distance. No embrace. She kissed him on both cheeks in a European style and pulled back, gripping his hands tightly. He looked down into her eyes, and he saw her then as she really was.

His damsel in distress.

Hazzim had finished his conversation and come quickly over.

"Eleni!"

Edwin clenched his jaw as the young man kissed her on both cheeks in a slow, lingering manner.

"You two know each other?" he asked, turning to Edwin with surprise.

Adriana answered quickly. "We met when I was in London doing my research," she explained. "In the summer."

"Ah," he said, nodding. "I'm surprised you didn't tell me!" he scolded her. "I love this guy."

Hazzim playfully punched Edwin on the shoulder.

"Mr. Talki?" he asked the manager. "Are we ready?"

"Yes, yes, Meester Nejem," the manager replied. "All is prepared." He turned to the butler and snapped his fingers quickly and dramatically, uttering commands in brisk Turkish. The butler hurried out of the room and returned with several more servants, each with trays of food.

"Let us eat!" announced Hazzim, gathering his guests to the table.

The meal was served in courses, each one surmounting the next. Stews, stuffed peppers and fish, rich sauces, spicy meats. The main course was served in individual covered dishes of silver shaped like pointed domes.

Edwin glanced at his host, sitting beside him at the head of the table, beaming down on his guests like a genial sultan. But Edwin could feel something sinister beneath the veneer of the perfect host. It meant power to Hazzim, control. He was the great provider of luxury, of opulence, but at what price to those who partook of his offerings? Edwin shuddered.

He looked across at Adriana. She had been looking at him, but quickly looked away.

"I missed you today, Eleni!" said Hazzim to Adriana, caressing her bare arm. "Why do you have to do that research? It's no fun!"

"You know I have to, Hazzim," she said, smiling at him. "But you need to explain to poor Edwin why you call me Eleni. He knows me as Adriana."

"It was Mr Talki's doing!" said Hazzim, indicating the manager sitting on the other side of Adriana.

Mr. Talki beamed. "Yes, yes. It was I who first called her that. *Eleni.* Helen. We were talking of Helen of Troy. What would the real Helen have looked like? I said, she would look like Mees Adriana. A dark-haired beauty with sunshine in her eyes! She is our *Eleni tis Troias*. Helen of Troy!"

Hazzim laughed, as if Adriana's beauty were his prize, his possession.

Edwin forced himself to smile with him.

Play your part.

"Do you not think, Meester Sterling?" asked Mr. Talki, his eyes twinkling. "Is she not the face that launched a thousand ships?"

Edwin kept smiling, put on the spot. He gazed across the table to where she sat studying him, leaning her chin on her hand in the same way she had in the Bella Luna. He could hear her voice in his head. "I'm trying to figure you out."

"Yes," he said simply, earnestly.

Had she not brought him here?

Hazzim gave him another punch on the arm.

"Only this time, no Paris will get her away from this King!" He laughed uproariously at his own joke. So did the rest of the table.

"Hazzim," said Adriana, teasingly. "You have no claim on me."

"Not yet, perhaps," he said, kissing her hand. She smiled at him in a way Edwin didn't like.

The evening seemed never-ending. Hazzim dominated the room, and paid particular attention to Adriana.

Mr. Talki left after the meal, bowing and smiling and hoping everything was to Meester Nejem's satisfaction, and the English couple left soon after.

Hazzim had settled himself comfortably on one of the sofas in the grand sitting room. The software company owner was right: he loved an audience. He told story after story about himself. Edwin's stomach began to feel nauseated, but he wasn't sure if it was the rich food or an overdose of another man's ego.

Toward midnight, Edwin began to feel the exhaustion from his sleepless night. He stood to leave.

"I'm afraid I am feeling the jet lag coming on," he said apologetically to the group. "If you'll excuse me, I really must get back to my room."

To his surprise, Adriana also stood. "Look at the time!" she said, consulting her watch. "And I have to get up early tomorrow."

"So soon, *inayyi*?" asked Hazzim.

"I have to go to work," she reminded him.

"Always working," he said plaintively.

"You have a job here?" asked Edwin, surprised.

"Just more research. Like I did in England. I've been going to the Archaeological Museums most days. I've almost finished. Then to finish writing the book I'm working on."

"You work too hard, Eleni," said Hazzim. "I will walk you to your room."

"No, that's not necessary, Hazzim," she said. "I believe Edwin is in the same part of the hotel. Do you mind, Edwin?"

"Not at all," he replied.

Hazzim stood up and took Adriana's hands.

"Until tomorrow then, *inayyi*," he said, kissing her cheek.

He turned to shake Edwin's hand.

"So glad to have met you. We will see you tomorrow, yes?"

"Well, I suppose so," said Edwin.

If I haven't gut-punched you.

Edwin should have been glad to finally have time alone with Adriana, but now the moment had come, he dreaded it.

She waited to speak until they had turned a corner and were out of earshot of the rather large, tough-looking Bahrainian who had followed them out and stood just outside the door of the Sultan's Suite.

Bodyguard, I'm assuming.

Even then, she chatted only about unimportant things, signaling him to wait to speak of anything else until they arrived at her room. Checking the hall first, she pulled him in and shut the door behind him.

"What are you doing here?" she demanded, her eyes flashing. "You aren't supposed to know where I am!"

Edwin reached inside his jacket and pulled out the newspaper photograph.

"A person who doesn't want to be found shouldn't have dinner with the most eligible bachelor in Bahrain," he demanded.

She snatched the newspaper from him. She studied it, her face smoldering, then pushed it back at him.

"He's a close-talker," she explained quickly, turning away.

"Adriana, I need to know the truth. What are you doing here in Istanbul?"

"I can't tell you."

"I've come all this way, and that's all you can say? You can't tell me?"

"You aren't supposed to be here."

"Is he the reason?"

"What?"

"Hazzim. Is he the reason you can only be my friend? The man standing between us?"

She hesitated for the briefest of a moment before replying.

"Yes. He is." She raised her eyes and looked at him steadily, defiantly.

No. Too steady.

"I don't believe you."

He began to move toward her. She jumped, like a frightened animal.

"Edwin! Don't make this more complicated than it already is."

She crossed the room, positioning herself behind a chair, gripping the back of it with white knuckles.

"Go home, Edwin. Please. I don't want to see you get hurt."

"Oh, that's so kind of you. To think of my feelings. Like you did when you left, and wouldn't tell me where you were going? Were you thinking of my feelings then?"

"There are things that you don't understand," she said.

"Tell me. Trust me!"

"I do trust you, Edwin. Too much."

She sighed heavily, as if she were carrying a great weight upon her shoulders.

"Go, Edwin," she said. "Go far away from me."

He wanted to run to her, to take her in his arms and leave Istanbul, leave England, leave everyone.

"I'll go to bed, Adriana. But that's all I'll promise."

29

Edwin slept late the next morning. It was partly due to jet lag, but the questions in his mind had kept him awake far longer than he wished. When he got up, he ordered breakfast from his butler, and decided he could get used to that.

He had gone to bed angry. Angry at Adriana. Angry at Hazzim. Angry at himself. He even threw Phillip into it. Why did he have to find that stupid photograph? *Wouldn't I be better off without knowing where she is? Without knowing the truth?*

But that's when the questions began coming. Because he didn't know the truth.

Edwin knew the wise thing to do at this point would be to leave. Cut his losses. It's what she said she wanted. But something deep within him wouldn't let him do the wise thing. The safe thing.

Something deep within him told him she needed him, and that somehow he had to stay, to stick it out.

She isn't Mary Alice Rowan. Hazzim isn't Stephen Quinn. And this time, I won't fade into the background like some kind of stage prop.

This time, I'll take the center.

He'd remembered, despite his haste in leaving town, to bring the script with him that Debra wanted him to read. He flipped through it. It was based on a popular novel about a lawyer trying to get a convicted murderer off of death row, while the real murderer, Edwin's character if he chose to play it, was trying to prevent him from doing so. It was gritty; it was suspenseful; it was probably the next big hit. Edwin was thankful he had something to occupy his brain while he waited for Adriana to come back from work.

Work. His mind began spinning again. What does she really do? That was one of the nagging questions that had kept him up the night before. All this research. Lengthy stays in foreign countries. Staying at the Ciragan Palace instead of something less expensive and nearer to the Museum. Who's paying for all of this? Hazzim?

Edwin shuddered at the thought.

He texted Phillip, letting him know things were not going well, but he was determined to stay.

Brenda sent him a photograph of Chloe.

Just thought you'd like to see this!

Chloe was standing, looking at the camera with a feigned look of surprise on her face. Simon, Edwin's director friend who had brought Chloe to the birthday party, was on his knee in front of her with a ring.

Wow. I wonder how long *that* will last?

Late in the afternoon, he strolled down to the Gazebo restaurant for tea. He was surprised once again by the lack of recognition from the other guests. Even the staff, who treated him well, did not look at him any differently than they did the other guests. To them, he was merely a well-paying patron.

Anonymity.

It had been so long since he had felt it. In school growing up he had felt it. Despite being Portia Valentine's or Sir Thomas' son, he was just one of the boys. Surrounded by young men like Phillip, the sons of earls, the sons of foreign dignitaries, nobody cared who his parents were. Except Mary Alice.

For years, as a struggling actor, nobody recognized him in the street or asked for his autograph in the airport. There were no screaming teenaged girls or crazy fans with knives. But success had stolen anonymity.

On the one hand, he grieved for it and was relieved to be left alone again, to be treated like everyone else. On the other hand, he was thankful for a full schedule, a successful career. Recognition. But fame is a fickle thing. How long would he have, he wondered, before he was forgotten? Ten years, five years, one? How long until the next Edwin Sterling came along?

He ambled down the great staircase behind the hotel to the garden that overlooked the Bosphorus. The water side of the Ciragan was famous for its beautiful double staircase that led from the river to the entrance to the hotel lobby above. Both sides of the ornately-decorated stone-carved stairs were carpeted in red, giving the appearance of a royal welcome.

Edwin passed the two outdoor pools, brilliantly blue. There were a few swimmers brave enough to swim in the heated infinity pool beside the Bosphorus. Palm trees stood like sentinels on either side of a beautiful fountain, and a great stone archway framed the walk that led up from the river. Guests could arrive and depart by boat here. A river cruise was just boarding; Edwin stood leaning against the cool stone of the arch, watching families and couples boarding the elaborately decorated golden boat. Their laughter echoed across the water long after they had departed.

Happiness. Such a transient thing.

He focused again on the dock, where another boat had arrived. This one was not so elaborate; it was small and white, with a bright blue hull.

Water taxi.

Only one passenger disembarked. Edwin was surprised to see it was Adriana. She was wearing a gold-colored scarf draped loosely over her hair, which she removed as she got off the boat. He was struck by how much she seemed to belong here. Like an Ottoman princess.

"Waiting for me?" she asked as she approached. She seemed tired and strained.

"Not intentionally," he said. "I didn't expect you to come and go by boat."

He joined her as she walked slowly toward the hotel.

"I prefer going by water taxi," she explained. "It's cooler, and there's less traffic."

They walked in silence, enjoying the breeze that washed up from the river. She began to relax, closing her eyes sometimes and breathing deep, slow breaths. He recognized the technique; he used it often to prepare for a part.

As they ascended the great staircase, she smiled weakly at him.

"I knew you wouldn't leave. You are so stubborn."

"I'm afraid you're right," he agreed. "But stubbornness can be a virtue. If you're stubborn for the right reasons, people call it being steadfast."

She smiled.

"Will you have dinner with us again?" she asked. "We're eating in the hotel restaurant tonight. Tugra. The one with the covered terrace."

"Will your boyfriend mind?"

"He's not my boyfriend, and I think he will be disappointed if you don't. He's a big fan of yours."

Once again, Edwin found himself across the table from Adriana, with Hazzim dominating the head of the table between them. The open air of the restaurant made it less stifling than in Hazzim's suite, where everything felt controlled by him. Here there were other hotel guests at other tables, evidence that everything did not revolve around the Bahrainian heir.

There was an indoor section of the restaurant, but on fair nights like this one, guests could eat on the covered terrace that overlooked the river. The breeze from the Bosphorus was cool and refreshing, and smelled slightly of the sea.

This evening Hazzim had condescended to ask about Edwin, his work, his future expectations. Edwin mentioned life as Dr. Hanover and told funny stories from the set. He even talked about the new script he was reading, in confidential tones. Once, Edwin looked up to find Adriana paying particular attention to him, though when Hazzim told stories, she often seemed far away, as if her thoughts were elsewhere.

"Say your famous line, Edwin," urged Hazzim. "Say 'It's a matter of life and death'!"

It was one of Dr. Hanover's iconic sayings. Edwin

tilted his head suavely to the side.

"It's a matter of life and death," he said in his serious Dr. Hanover voice.

Hazzim clapped and laughed uproariously.

"That's so great! I love it!"

He gave Edwin an appreciative slap on the shoulder.

"So what about this Chloe, Edwin?" asked Hazzim, out of the blue.

Mortifying.

"It looked like you two had a thing going. Now I see she's engaged to someone else."

He eyed Edwin with a steady gaze.

Looking for something to hold over my head.

He could feel the attention of the entire table; Edwin shrugged and shook his head.

"It was nothing," he admitted.

That's the truth.

"She was a beautiful distraction. Nothing more," he added, choosing to endear himself to Hazzim by his detachment. "I wish her all the happiness she deserves."

He glanced quickly at Adriana, wondering how much she knew, how she felt.

Her face was impassive, like stone.

Toward the end of the meal, Hazzim's silent butler approached and whispered something in his ear.

"Excellent! Thank you, Bahadir," said Hazzim. He turned excitedly to Adriana.

"So, it is settled, Eleni," he announced. "Tomorrow we go to Canakkale."

Adriana shifted uncomfortably in her chair, glancing at Edwin.

"Come with us, Edwin!" Hazzim cried, his arms outstretched, as if he were offering something for sale. "We go to Canakkale for the day. Eleni wants to see the city of Troy. Helen visiting Troy!" He laughed.

"You're changing hotels?" asked Edwin, surprised.

"No, no. No need. My plane is here in Istanbul. We will go to Troy and come back to Istanbul in one day. Every Englishman wants to see Troy!"

"I thought it would just be us, Hazzim," said Adriana, pouting.

"*Inayyi!* We cannot be selfish! There's always room for one more in my party."

Edwin hesitated.

"Don't you have to leave tomorrow, Edwin?" Adriana asked, her eyebrows raised.

A challenge.

"No. I have no plans to leave just yet," he replied, meeting her gaze.

"Excellent." Hazzim clapped his hands together as if closing a deal.

30

It was a small party going to Canakkale. Edwin guessed that Hazzim had five "friends" with him at the Ciragan, though some of them looked more like security. Two of them were going with them to visit Troy. Adriana would have been disappointed, even if he had refused the invitation. She would not have been alone with Hazzim.

The Ciragan had a helipad on site, so of course, Hazzim had arranged for transportation to the airport via helicopter. They would then transfer to his private plane for travel to Canakkale.

Pretentious.

At least it would lessen the travel time. Edwin was dreading what he knew would be the never-ending Hazzim show.

On a whim, Edwin had emailed Phillip to ask if Mr. Tastan lived in Istanbul. Phillip's research said that Kara Inci's headquarters were in Kirikkale, a good five hours from Istanbul and farther than that from Troy. For some reason, Edwin felt relieved.

At Troy they took a guided tour. Edwin was fascinated; this ancient city of legend and myth actually existed, and here he was, walking on the walls and gazing on the tombs of ancient warriors. The city itself was actually multiple cities, built and rebuilt on top of each other over thousands of years. The Troy of the Iliad was guessed to be the seventh city of Troy, where archaeology showed evidence of fire and great battle.

As the group stood standing at the edge of the city, gazing out across the flat fields beyond, Edwin couldn't help but think of the conversation between his father and Adriana. They had talked of Troy.

"Danger and mystery," Edwin said out loud.

Adriana shivered beside him.

"I just got goosebumps," she said, rubbing her arms. "Isn't it amazing to think that this view, this flat field where the Greeks and Trojans fought, looks the same as it did then? We're looking at rocks and land that saw battle after battle. Thousands of years of bloodshed."

They all stared at the fields, thinking of Paris and King Menelaus, warriors fighting hand to hand and on chariots. Even Hazzim was silent for once.

"And for what, really?" asked Edwin. "What were they really fighting for?"

"Jealousy," said Adriana. "Envy, selfishness. Just like always."

"In this case, it was about a beautiful woman, eh, *inayyi*?" said Hazzim, his eyes twinkling at Adriana. "Helen of Troy."

She laughed. "Maybe. But isn't it more than that? Isn't it always more than that?"

She walked away, heading up to the top of the hill behind them.

Hazzim and Edwin stayed, still staring at the fields.

Standing their ground.

Edwin thought about what she said. The stories said it was love and passion that caused the Trojan war. Jealousy over a woman.

"Honor," said Hazzim, as if answering his thoughts. He looked at Edwin. "A king has to fight for his honor. The honor of his people."

He nodded his head as if satisfied with his own answer.

Arrogant. He thinks he's a king.

Honor, thought Edwin. Jealousy, selfishness. Isn't it always more than that, she asks. Maybe.

But sometimes, sometimes it's simply about the love of a woman.

He turned to look for her. She was standing at the top of the hill, at the area considered to be the location of King Priam's palace. Where Queen Helen may have stood long ago, watching the battle. She did look like Helen, a Mediterranean Queen, her dark hair streaming behind her in the breeze. She was looking into the distance, like she was seeing that battle, or countless centuries of battles. No fear in her eyes right now. Only sadness. 'There's always danger in war, no matter which side you're on,' he heard his father's voice say. And Adriana had said, 'It's part of the risk.'

Hazzim followed his gaze.

"Mm-mm," he said to Edwin under his breath. "The beautiful Eleni, Queen of my heart."

"Is she?" Edwin asked without thinking.

"For now," he answered, smiling.

Edwin glanced at Hazzim out of the corner of his eye.

He looks like a spider. Spinning his web and leering at her from the middle of it.

I want to crush him under my foot.

They ate lunch that had been brought as a picnic from the hotel. Afterward, Hazzim received a text and suddenly announced that he needed to meet someone. He took his two fellow Bahrainians with him.

"Here?" Adriana asked. "In the middle of nowhere?"

"A friend from Canakkale," he explained. "Just business. I won't be long, *inayyi*," he said to her. She pretended to be sorry to part from him. Or was she really sorry?

They watched Hazzim cross to the ruins some distance away. A man met him, shrouded in the shadow of a large rocky piece of wall.

Edwin glanced at Adriana, who was watching the proceedings intently. He couldn't imagine she could seriously consider the affections of this egocentric spoiled brat. Certainly he noticed, or thought he did, her patience waning. But if she really is a gold-digger, if she really is only after a wealthy husband, like Phillip suggested—another Mary Alice—then...

But he couldn't think of that.

The two of them were sitting in the theatre of Troy, built by the Romans during a later period of the city's history.

Naturally, the theatre. Don't I feel at home here?

Always playing a part.

Although it was autumn, the sun was bright and hot. The little shade there was in the almost treeless expanse was shading a small section of the theatre seats that terraced up the hill. So there they sat, Adriana and Edwin. Waiting.

Adriana relaxed after a few minutes and began to appear completely at ease, almost happy, as she sat beside him. She had stopped watching Hazzim so closely and seemed content to wait. Waiting. Like a fly caught in a web.

She says she trusts me. And Hazzim is a spider.

"Adriana, about Hazzim," he began.

She held up her hand. "I don't want to talk about Hazzim."

"How did you meet?"

She rolled her eyes, but gave in. "We met at the hotel. Mr. Talki introduced us."

"And you just—hit it off?"

"Hazzim is a handsome, intelligent man. Any woman would fall for him." Her gaze returned to the young man speaking animatedly near the ruins.

"Have you?"

She looked him fully in the face.

Pity. She feels sorry for me.

"Edwin, I told you to leave. You'll only get hurt here."

"I'm a grown man, Adriana. You don't have to spare my feelings."

She laughed haughtily.

"Like you spared mine last night? Chloe is just a beautiful distraction?"

He was stunned by her intensity. Is she jealous?

"You left," he sputtered. "You wouldn't tell me where you were going. And all the while it was here, with—"

"I looked it up, Edwin. You had her lipstick all over you."

There were tears in her eyes. The shame of using Chloe for revenge stung him.

"We only kissed," he said, grabbing her hand. She pulled it away.

"I swear, Adriana," he insisted. "We only kissed. I thought she would make the pain go away. I used her. I admit it. It was stupid. But she can't even compare to you. Please believe me."

But she wouldn't speak any more about it. She stared out again over the ruined city.

"Whatever I've done, it's not worth using him to get back at me," he said.

She remained silent.

"I just don't think he's all you think he is," Edwin said finally.

"I know what I'm doing," she replied, setting her jaw.

She seemed able to turn her emotions on and off like a faucet. Edwin was beginning to wonder if her moments of passion were unintentional glimpses into her soul or if they were calculated, a means to an end.

He pulled at a piece of grass growing up between the stones.

Change the subject.

"I've been meaning to ask you," he began, remembering one of his nagging questions. "Do you know Mr. Tastan?"

She furrowed her brow.

"Know him personally?"

Edwin shrugged. "I thought you might have met him before. At the Museum."

"No. I never met him."

"Someone saw you at the Swan that day. The day of the attempted bombing. They thought you might have been visiting him there."

"They must have been mistaken," she said cooly.

"Maybe."

"Who was it? Who says they saw me?"

Edwin shrugged. "Someone I met."

Her eyes narrowed suspiciously.

"Do they think I was involved somehow in the bombing?" she asked. "Do you?"

"I just wondered—"

"Seriously, Edwin. How would I know someone like Mr. Tastan? And why would I bring him a bomb in his tea?"

"Forget I mentioned it," Edwin said.

"I was with you that day," she added quietly.

"I remember."

They sat silently for a few minutes, neither one wanting to speak. They could see Hazzim beginning to cross over the walls of Troy toward them.

"Edwin," said Adriana earnestly. "Don't mention Mr. Tastan again. Especially in front of Hazzim. Kara Inci is a rival, and Hazzim can be very jealous."

31

The rest of the trip was uneventful. Edwin napped on the flight back to Istanbul. They arrived around dinnertime, and after changing, ate once again in the beautiful Tugra restaurant. After dinner, the party moved to the bar in the lobby. It was brightly lit, and open to the Atrium with its burgundy marble tiles. Adriana only stayed for one drink.

"It's been a long day," she explained as she stood to leave. "Hazzim, would you like to go into the city tomorrow? I wanted to visit the Spice Bazaar, and you know I leave in just two days."

"Oh, so sorry, Eleni!" he said apologetically. "Tomorrow I have a meeting. I will be gone all day."

He caressed her hand and pulled her closer to him.

"But I will make it up to you. Will you have dinner with me tomorrow night?" he asked. "Just the two of us. In my suite."

She giggled.

Edwin's stomach churned.

"Okay," she said, her eyelids fluttering as she smiled coyly at him.

Hazzim kissed her hand.

"Tomorrow, Eleni," he said with a sultry smile. He ogled her shapely form as she walked away toward the Atrium staircases.

Sickening.

"So, not tonight, I guess, Hazzim!" teased one of his friends.

Hazzim laughed and shrugged. "Not tonight. This one is making me work for it." He sighed. "A long time I've been working for this prize. But I think she will be worth it."

He laughed again, slapping Edwin affectionately on the shoulder.

"You know how it is, Edwin," he said. "These American women, they are so stupid. Give them a little foreign accent and a little savoir faire and they are putty in your hands."

Edwin could feel the heat surging through him. He clenched his fist.

We are not the same.

"But this one, she is smarter than most," Hazzim continued. "It takes more time. But I shall have her in the end."

"So, you intend to marry her?" asked Edwin.

"Marry her?" Hazzim laughed derisively. "I just need her in my bed. And I think I am close now. Very close. But, in the meantime—"

Edwin followed his gaze to a blonde young woman seated at the bar. She smiled seductively at Hazzim, who walked over to her.

"Wish me luck, my friend," he said with a grin.

I hate spiders.

Edwin sat in stunned silence. He returned his attention to the Atrium where Adriana had disappeared. *Does she know her handsome Bahrainian is a player? Does she care?*

But something else ended his silent reverie.

There were two staircases in the Atrium that curved upward to the Mezzanine. Adriana had climbed one of the staircases and had just disappeared toward her room. Edwin noticed a dark-haired man wearing a mustache and a hotel uniform warily staring after her. Then, after furtively glancing around, he also ascended the stairs. When he reached the Mezzanine, the man continued to follow Adriana toward the old palace rooms.

Edwin sat thoughtfully in his chair. He sipped his drink, but a knot began to form in the pit of his stomach. Something wasn't right. He didn't like the looks of that man; his face had a serious determination about it. And as far as Edwin knew, their small party were the only guests in the older part of the hotel.

No, something isn't right.

He rose and ascended the grand staircase. Adrenaline rushed through him with every step. As he turned toward the old palace suites, he realized he didn't have an actual plan.

If Adriana is in danger, what am I going to do?

He patted his pockets, as if expecting some phantom weapon to have magically materialized.

He was at her door. There was no one in the hall. Edwin stepped closer to the door, straining for any sound. He could hear voices talking, arguing he thought. They were speaking in Turkish, a man and a woman.

He took a deep breath and knocked on the door.

The voices stopped abruptly.

"Adriana?" he called out. "It's Edwin."

There was no reply.

"Adriana? Are you all right?"

He heard scuffling and a woman's muffled cry.

Without thinking, Edwin tried the door. It was unlocked. He threw it open to find Adriana struggling in the arms of the man in hotel uniform, who was forcibly kissing her. Edwin charged at him, pushing them apart. The man quickly dropped his hold on Adriana, grabbed Edwin, restraining him from behind, and pressed a large knife against his throat. Edwin struggled to breathe, his life flashing across his mind as he watched Adriana screaming something and holding out her hands in a stopping motion.

"No! He's exactly who he says he is!"

What does she mean? Why is everything in slow motion? How is it possible to relive my entire life in this split second of time?

Edwin's mind snapped back into reality, and time began again.

The dark-haired man laughed derisively, shoving him toward Adriana, who clung to him, touching his throat where the knife had been pressed.

The man sneered something in Turkish.

"Get out," Adriana said dismissively.

He obeyed, sneering as he closed the door behind him.

Adriana turned her attention to Edwin, tenderly touching his throat again.

"Are you hurt?" she asked anxiously.

"I'm fine. Are you all right? Did he hurt you?" Edwin cradled her face in his hands.

"He didn't hurt me," she assured him.

He crossed the room and picked up the hotel telephone on a table by the door.

"Where's your butler?" he asked.

"I dismissed him for the night. Don't!" she cried, hanging up the receiver.

"We have to call the front desk!" he said, incredulous. "We need them to call the police!"

"No. He didn't do any harm."

"He tried to kill me!" Edwin stared at her in disbelief.

Is she in shock?

"I don't understand," he said. "I found him trying to molest you."

"No. He heard you at the door and thought you were an enemy. He pretended to kiss me so you would come in to the room and he could identify you. He was protecting me. From you."

Edwin clutched the sides of his head, trying to keep his mind from exploding.

"Who are you?" he asked.

Her chest heaved up and down as if her breathing were labored.

"I can't tell you," she said finally.

"And I'm supposed to accept that?" he asked, raising his voice.

"I've never lied to you, Edwin," she pleaded. "I just haven't told you everything."

"Can you now?"

"No."

They stood staring at one another.

"What did he say to you, as he left?" he asked.

"Nothing," she said. "Something stupid."

"You speak Turkish?"

"My mother was Turkish," she replied defiantly.

"What did he say?" His tone was angry, almost menacing.

"He said he doesn't know what I see in you, and that I'd be better off with him."

Edwin nodded. "And what do you see? In me."

She studied every inch of his face before she spoke.

"I see the bravest man I've ever known."

Pulling him toward her, she kissed him.

"I need you to do this one thing for me," she whispered, her lips hovering close to his.

Anything.

"I need you to trust me. Can you do that?"

Edwin looked deeply into her eyes. Sunshine in her eyes, Mr. Talki had said.

"Yes."

32

The next morning, Edwin decided to get up early and eat breakfast in Laledan, which served a breakfast buffet on the ground floor of the hotel. From his table on the terrace, he could look down into the palm garden below. Since Hazzim wouldn't be around, he was hoping to catch Adriana on her way into the city.

As he sipped his coffee, his mind reflected on the events of the night before. Since arriving in Istanbul, Adriana had played his feelings like a yo-yo, pushing him away and then pulling him close with a look, a kiss.

A kiss.

And last night he had promised to trust her. But he still didn't know why. Trust her in what?

His phone, which was lying on the table, vibrated the silverware.

Hello. This is your mother millicent taught me how to text where r u?

Brilliant.

He checked his messages. There was one from Jen. "Sorry to bother you, but Debra wanted me to remind you about the script. I hope you're reading it, Edwin."

A waiter carrying a tray of dishes had paused beside a palm tree in the garden below. His lack of movement caught Edwin's attention; he looked down to find the waiter staring at him. It was the mustachioed hotel employee from the night before! He gave Edwin a half sneer, then moved on.

He wanted me to see him. To know he's watching.

I am exactly who I say I am.

Who else would I be? Who is she?

As if on cue, Adriana appeared, dressed for the city. She saw Edwin and came over.

"Going into the city?" he asked.

Obvious.

"Would you like to come?" she asked, almost shyly, as if he might refuse.

They took a water taxi. Adriana donned her scarf again. She wore it loosely, more as a show of respect than a true covering.

"I wish I could show you the Topkapi Palace or Hagia Sophia," she said as they sped along the Bosphorus, "but we don't have time today. Today we shop!"

The Grand Bazaar was an experience Edwin knew he would never forget. Open since the 1400's, its rows and rows of stalls and vendors were housed in mosaic-tiled archways. In it was sold anything and everything you could imagine: intricately woven Turkish carpets, piles of exotic foods, silver wares, copper wares, and coffee. Glorious Turkish coffee.

It was crowded with locals and tourists, and was loud with bartering and greetings and laughter. The air was thick with garlic, body odor, curry and peppers.

In one section, the throng of people was so dense, they had to squeeze their way through. Edwin was surprised to feel Adriana's hand slip into his.

So we don't get separated.

But afterward, she didn't let go. They walked hand-in-hand through the bazaar, stopping to look, to taste, to buy. They lunched, standing at an outdoor counter, on marinated beef on a bed of something Adriana insisted would be good. Edwin didn't know what it was, but she was right. After several hours of walking and exploring, she led him to the Spice Bazaar.

He could smell it long before they arrived. The aromas were exhilarating. Candy-colored powdered spices were displayed in jars and bowls. There were piles of olives and dates. One vendor sold creams and lotions with heavenly scents. Teas of all sorts, from strong black teas to flowery jasmine and herbals, were sold by the pound.

Turkish tea.

But Adriana did not buy any, in a canister or otherwise.

When she did stop, it was to admire a colorful display of scented bath salts under an archway. The young man in the shop wore a turban of rolled linen.

"Oh! How lovely!" she exclaimed, choosing a jar and smelling its contents. She put it up to Edwin's nose. He sneezed.

She laughed.

"Sorry! How much for this?" she asked the young man.

He named a price. She bargained for a lower price.

"For you, pretty lady, I agree. What scent would you like? This pink is rose petal and the blue is lavender and lemon balm."

"Which do you suggest?" she asked.

"Blue is my best-seller," he replied, handing one to her.

"Thank you," she said, paying him.

They had tea in a local place Adriana knew. She seemed completely at ease, as if the weight she had been carrying had been removed. Edwin wasn't sure what to think about it, but he didn't want it to end. This was how it felt in the beginning, when they had first met. Before Istanbul. Before Hazzim. Before "friendship" had become the order of the day. They had simply enjoyed each other's company; they had been happy, like the photograph had shown. He wished they could stay just like this, in this moment, far from the confusion their lives had become. Far from the nagging questions and the inadequate explanations.

But then, that wouldn't be the truth.

As they rose to leave, Adriana accidentally dropped her purse onto the floor, spilling the contents. Edwin chased a lipstick. When he tried to put it back into her purse, she snatched it quickly from his hand and stuffed it into the partially opened bag, but not before he caught a glimpse of something unusual inside.

"Is that a gun?" he asked, trying to keep his voice down despite his surprise.

She looked up sharply.

"No. It's a taser."

"You have a taser?" he asked.

"Well, single girl, foreign country. Yes, I have a taser."

"How did you get it past security?"

She shrugged.

"It's easier than you think."

She threw in a compact and snapped her bag shut.

"Come on, or we'll miss our taxi."

On the boat ride back to the hotel, Edwin received a text from Phillip.

Call me ASAP

He wondered what the urgency was about. Had something happened to one of his parents? He had a sinking feeling in his stomach that he knew wasn't seasickness.

The closer they got to the Ciragan, the wider the distance grew between him and Adriana. Although they hadn't moved from their seats, hadn't physically changed positions, emotionally she was miles away from him again, and the weight of her invisible burden settled once more about her shoulders like the scarf that covered her. He wished he could carry it for her, whatever it was.

For some reason, he couldn't get the taser out of his mind. In a way, it made sense: it was for protection. But protection from whom?

They disembarked and headed for the curving stairs. Mr. Talki stood at the top balcony. He beamed his greeting when he saw them.

"Meester Sterling! Mees Adriana! I hope you had a pleasant time in the city?" he said as they approached him.

"Yes, of course, Mr. Talki," Adriana said. His quick eyes appraised her.

"You seem weary, Eleni," he said with concern.

"All is well," she assured him.

"Everything is prepared for tonight," he said. "For dinner with Meester Nejem."

"Thank you, Mr. Talki," she said.

Edwin clenched his jaw.

The spider's web is ready.

She turned to him.

"Thank you for coming with me, Edwin. It was good to spend time together again."

Although her mouth was smiling, her eyes were impassive, impenetrable. She kissed him quickly on the cheek before leaving the two men on the balcony.

They watched her retreat. Mr. Talki turned to Edwin.

"You and Eleni, you are good friends?" he asked.

Good friends? Be a good friend.

He sighed, slowly and bitterly.

"Yes," was his simple reply.

He went back to his room. *Tonight is the night. Adriana having dinner with Hazzim, alone. And I am to trust her.*

But I don't trust him.

He remembered Phillip's text and picked up his phone.

Phillip's voice sounded tense and excitable.

"Edwin, good. Thank you for calling me back," he said, relieved.

"What's up?" asked Edwin.

"I've been speaking to Jeff. Edwin, you've got to get out of there."

"Why?"

"It's dangerous. This whole thing is—out of control."

"Phillip, what are you talking about?"

"Look, you know I've been asking questions about your mystery woman, so when I told Jeff we'd found her and where you'd gone, he got kind of freaked out. Apparently, the Bahrain Oil Company and Kara Inci have a pretty intense rivalry."

"Yeah. Adriana mentioned that."

"Jeff says, and you can't quote him on this, but he says they strongly suspect that the attempts on Mr. Tastan's life can be linked back to Hazzim Nejem and BOC."

Edwin was silent.

"Ed? Are you still there?"

"Yes."

"Jeff says Mr. Tastan has another public appearance in New York in three days' time. They're probably planning another attempt. So you've got to get out of there. If Hazzim Nejem is involved in this, then—"

"Then what?" Edwin snapped.

Just shut up and let me think.

"Then Adriana must be working for him. It's the only thing that makes sense. And if that's true—Edwin, you're in grave danger!"

"Is there any other kind?" Edwin quoted.

"This is serious. Why would you quote *A Few Good Men* at a time like this?

"I don't know. It just doesn't seem real."

He sat at the table in his room, trying to make sense out of what he had just learned. Adriana working for Hazzim? Is that even possible? Is that why she feels obligated to be romantic with him? If he wants it, then she risks her life to refuse. She needs me to save her.

Why would I save her? A woman who works for a terrorist? A woman who lies, who protects a terrorist, who carries around a taser, who—surely not. Surely she doesn't kill for him? Would she kill for a man she loves?

She's not a killer.

Edwin struggled to calm his mind.

Think. Think back.

She comes to England at the same time as Mr. Tastan. Someone tries to shoot him, and Adriana is in the Museum at the time. What was her role? To usher in the shooter? Put him in the balcony?

A bomb is planted in Mr. Tastan's flat, and Adriana

is seen exiting the building on the very day.

"Do you think I brought him a bomb in his tea?" she said just yesterday. Phillip said it wasn't in the papers that it was in the tea canister. How else would she know unless she was there?

"*I was with you that day.*" Out of breath to meet me. Am I her alibi?

The crazy fan at Kensington. Was that a coincidence or something more? The constable said she was trained. Trained by whom to do what?

"Work" is the reason we have to be friends. "Work" is the reason she has to leave after my birthday party. Not history, but something very much in the present. Working for Hazzim.

Hazzim. The man between them.

If Hazzim is planning another attempt on Mr. Tastan's life, then maybe all these meetings—in Troy yesterday, somewhere else today—maybe he's setting things in motion. And all the while, his alibi is his continual vacation. He wasn't anywhere near Mr. Tastan.

But she was.

And she will be. She leaves in two days to go back to America. To New York, perhaps?

No wonder she was angry I came. I complicate things. And maybe, just maybe, she cares enough about me to fear for my life.

Fear in her eyes, fear of being recognized, photographed. Fear that I would find out who she was or what she was doing.

I am exactly who I say I am.

She saved my life from a mysterious hotel employee with a knife. He must also work for Hazzim. How far does this go? Can I trust anyone?

She asked me to trust her. What a fool I've been. Trust her! A murderer! A terrorist!

Well, I don't know that. Mr. Tastan is still alive. Maybe she's not a murderer.

Yet.

33

Edwin threw on a dinner jacket to go down for dinner, still dazed from his conversation with Phillip.

Dinner for one tonight.

He had taken the time to call Jen to book his flight home for the next day. He had no reason to stay, and as Phillip pointed out, a very good reason to leave.

He could tell Jen had a million questions, but she thankfully didn't ask them. He knew he owed her an explanation. But not yet.

As he stepped out into the hall, it was eerily quiet.

He glanced in both directions, but there was no one there. No threat.

Just my imagination.

He crossed through the Atrium, passing the stairway. There was a Turkish family at the front desk, checking in. A European businessman sat alone at the bar.

Nothing suspicious.

He continued on. As he approached the hostess stand of the restaurant, Mr. Talki intercepted him.

"Meester Sterling!"

Edwin jumped.

"So sorry, Meester Sterling! I did not mean to startle you."

"It's okay. I'm just a little on edge this evening."

"Only one tonight?"

"I'm afraid so."

"Perhaps Meester Sterling would like to make a reservation for later, eh? Perhaps Meester Sterling would like to take a walk in the rose garden before dinner?"

Perplexed, Edwin followed Mr. Talki's jerking head motions. Through the large open doors that led to the balcony of the Tugra he could see into the rose garden. A lone figure walked among the rows of bushes.

Adriana.

He only hesitated for a moment.

"Perhaps I *will* take a walk first," Edwin agreed.

"Yes, very wise. Always good to work up the appetite."

Romantic at heart, our Mr. Talki.

He wasn't sure what he was going to say to her. Despite Phillip's warnings, he still couldn't bring himself to fear her, no matter who her boyfriend was. No matter what she carried in her purse. Surely *she* wasn't a threat to him.

The rose garden was beyond the palm garden between the old and new sections of the hotel. There was a fountain in the center that dampened sound, making it feel more secluded than it actually was. Despite the lateness of the season, the rose garden was still in bloom. The moon was full and shimmered its silvery path across the waters of the Bosphorus.

Edwin paused. She was wearing her red dress again, the one with the rose on the shoulder, but the moonlight muted all colors into shades of gray; her silhouette was outlined in silver, like a ghostly figure, like something unreal.

Like a dream.

Or a memory.

"Can you smell them, Edwin?" she asked in a low, dreamy voice. She hadn't looked up when he approached; she spoke as if she expected him to be there.

She leaned over a particular flower and drew in its scent. Her hair was up this evening, and he could see the graceful curve of her neck.

Still beautiful.

"It reminds me of the roof garden," she said. "Remember? At the Début?"

"How could I forget?"

"I gave you a birthday kiss. And you told me you loved me."

It felt like she had stabbed a knife through his heart, but he pretended to be unmoved.

"You did hear me, then," he said.

"How could I not?" she whispered.

She stepped closer to him.

"It would have been better if we had never met, Edwin Sterling," she said, her eyes taking in every detail of his face. "Whatever happens tonight, please know that it was never my intention to hurt you."

To hurt me?

She looked away quickly when she heard the sound of voices. A yacht had just docked at the landing near the archway. It was Hazzim, returning, ready for his dinner. Ready for Adriana.

The spider, weaving his web, keeping his victim from escaping.

Maybe she can still be saved.

It was a risk. She could reject him, and just like with Mary Alice Rowan, everyone would know. Only this time, everyone would be more than just the guys at school; this time, everyone could mean the whole world. But he couldn't let her go without a fight.

There's always danger in war.

It's part of the risk.

"Adriana!" said Edwin, grabbing her arm. "Don't do it!"

She turned to him with widened, surprised eyes.

"Don't do what?"

Fear in her eyes again.

"Don't have dinner with him. Don't have any-thing more to do with him."

He was desperate; Hazzim was approaching quick-ly. He could see his jaunty, confident gait out of the corner of his eye. Just like Stephen Quinn. There was no more time.

"Why?" she asked, searching his face.

He hesitated. Trust her?

"Because he's a womanizer," he said. "A player. All he wants is—"

"Oh!" she sounded relieved. "Edwin, my sweet darling!"

She kissed him on the cheek.

"I have to do this."

"Eleni!" Hazzim called.

"Goodbye, Edwin."

She went to him obediently.

As if jealous of the scene he had just witnessed, Hazzim greeted her by kissing her lovingly on the lips instead of his usual European greeting. The friends with him hooted and egged him on. He grinned, glancing sideways at Edwin. Adriana smiled and laughed.

Another stab to the heart.

"Good evening, Edwin!" Hazzim said, waving an arm. "But I doubt yours will be quite as enjoyable as mine!"

Edwin managed to smile and wave.

"Have fun, kids," he said, jokingly, but inwardly he was dying.

I hope you choke on your gold chains.

Edwin cried.

If asked, he would blatantly deny it, but he did, in fact, cry.

Fortunately, being somewhat old-fashioned, he had a handkerchief in his pocket.

He knew the battle was lost. He had risked, and been defeated.

Hazzim had won.

He stayed in the rose garden for a full thirty minutes before going back up to the Tugra for dinner.

It was deathly quiet in the rose garden when he rose to leave; the bubbling fountain seemed to pull all sound within itself. As he passed from the rose garden to the palm garden, Edwin got the unnerving feeling of being watched. Palm fronds threw crazy shadows on the ground that waved in the breeze. He squinted, searching the shadows for any human movement, but there was none.

Grave danger, Phillip said.

As he neared the hotel, there were a few people milling about. The Turkish family who had just checked in were now at the pool, the children splashing and squealing. A young couple strolled along the edge of the Bosphorus, hand in hand. Edwin felt a little safer in company, but he still paused every now and then to look behind him.

Nothing.

Leaving the pool behind, he began to climb the steps to the door of the hotel.

Was that footsteps?

He paused, halfway up. No one. Only splashing from the family in the pool. He continued walking.

No. Definitely footsteps.

This time he could just make out a dim figure below him in the shadows where the architecture of the building formed a corner. He froze. The figure, as if waiting for him to notice, stepped into the light of one of the flood lamps.

It was the mustachioed hotel employee.

Their eyes locked for a moment. The man sneered at Edwin again, and he could hear him make a sound of disgust as he stepped once more into the shadows.

He wants me to see him, to fear him.

It's working.

Edwin raced up the four or five more steps to the hotel lobby and breathed a sigh of relief, thankful to put glass doors and full light between himself and the mustachioed menace below.

Once more at the Tugra restaurant, if Mr. Talki noticed any redness around Edwin's eyes, he respectfully did not comment. He seated him at a small table indoors, and Edwin was quite happy to not be on the terrace in full view of any mustachioed terrorists in the courtyard.

While at dinner, Edwin received another text from his mother.

Phillip says u r in Turkey your father says not very wise. R U OK?

Next I'll be getting little emoticons.

Edwin texted back that he was fine and would be returning home the next day. He didn't want to stay another moment.

Whether she's innocent of terrorism or not, she isn't innocent of Hazzim.

After dinner, Edwin had a drink, sitting at the bar in the lobby. It was a weeknight and the off-season, so Edwin was the only occupant, other than the bartender. Only the occasional guest passed through the Atrium on the way to his room.

Last night in Istanbul.

Last night with Adriana.

He closed his eyes.

How had it come to this? A chance meeting in the airport to international terrorism? Surely this is the stuff of fantasy. This isn't real life.

What is real?

What do I even mean when I say that? Edwin mused within himself, searching for the answer.

A real life is having someone who loves me for who I am, who I really am, not a character I play or an image someone created, or a stepping stone to someone else. But just as important, someone I can love for who she is, who she really is, someone who will trust me enough to show me that, and not hide behind a lie.

There was a commotion in the Atrium behind him. Through the mirror over the bar, Edwin could see a figure in red descending rapidly down the stairs. He turned on his stool.

Adriana, the rose of her dress falling limply off her shoulder, was storming down the stairs, followed by two of the Bahrainian young men, who were clearly trying to reason with her. Arms were flailing and voices were raised.

Mr. Talki, who had retired to an office on the ground floor of the lobby, came out to investigate the noise. He, too, began flailing his arms in a vain attempt to calm the situation.

Edwin stood and moved closer to the edge of the bar area to get a better view. As he watched the scene unfolding in front of him, he felt as if he were backstage, watching a play. Everything seemed in slow motion: Adriana, with her dress partially unzipped in the back revealing her bra strap, making cutting motions with her arms. Finality. The Bahrainians, looking dull-witted and confused, attempting to tell their side of whatever story was being played out. Mr. Talki, diplomatic, appeasing, ushering the group across the Atrium to his office. He looked around the lobby as he went, obviously hoping no other guests were witnessing the scene.

Before she followed, Adriana glanced over the limp rose on her shoulder to where Edwin was standing. She looked down and away, seemingly embarrassed. Straightening her shoulders, she walked with her head held high toward the manager's office.

Edwin's thoughts were wild and jutted in and out of his brain. Nothing made sense. He stared hard at the glass that was still in his hand, then put it down on a nearby table.

Another commotion at the top of the Atrium staircase.

This time it was Hazzim. He was being supported between two of his friends and was being half-carried down the stairs. He was pale and sweat was dripping across his forehead. His usually perfect hair was a mess, and his clothes were slightly disheveled, as if he had been in a fight. He almost looked drunk, but Edwin could tell that wasn't quite the right assumption. Every now and then, he favored what seemed to be a sore spot on his abdomen and groaned aloud.

He also went to the manager's office.

Edwin looked to the bartender for his assessment.

The bartender shrugged. "Lover's quarrel, I presume." He went back to wiping down the bar.

No, something more.

He waited. Curiosity was too strong to go to his room now.

He settled himself into one of the low tables and chairs at the edge of the bar. About fifteen minutes after Hazzim joined the group in the office, the meeting dispersed. Adriana, with her dress zipped and straightened, marched across the Atrium, her heels clicking rhythmically against the marble tiles. She didn't look in Edwin's direction, but went straight upstairs to her room.

She was followed, more slowly, by the Bahrainians. Hazzim was still being supported, but he was clearly recovering from whatever his ordeal had been. Instead of going upstairs, they descended on the bar and Edwin.

Hazzim collapsed into a low chair beside Edwin, his arms hanging limply at his sides in defeat. He reminded Edwin of a prize fighter who has lost his first fight. He still looked dazed, as if he was having trouble believing what had just happened.

Edwin remained silent, waiting for him to speak first.

Hazzim reached over and weakly slapped at Edwin's shoulder.

"Steer clear of that one, my friend," he said. "She is not worth the trouble."

"What happened?" Edwin ventured.

Hazzim rubbed his face with both his hands.

"She tasered me," he announced, as if still in shock.

"What?"

"I know! We had eaten a nice dinner, very romantic. I sent the butler away so we could be alone. We were kissing. It was—very nice," he said, as if remembering fondly. "Then she started saying no, like she didn't want to go further."

His anger was apparent.

"Hmm," Edwin grunted, smoldering.

The spider moving in on the prey.

"You know what these girls are like, Edwin," he said. "They say no, but they always mean yes. I thought she would give in, eventually. Then, out of nowhere, she pulls out a taser, and POW! ZAP! I'm on the ground. Can't move! Have you ever been tasered, Edwin?"

"No, I can't say I have."

"She hit me right here," he said, pointing to his abdomen. "Couldn't feel a thing after that. Couldn't think. Couldn't get up. I'm all curled up like a baby. It was in her purse. She pushed me off and grabbed it."

"Wow."

"I never saw it coming. The next thing I know, she's standing over me, yelling at me. Accusing me of trying to rape her and saying she was going down to tell Mr. Talki."

The pieces were beginning to fit together in Edwin's mind, but they still didn't make a clear picture. Didn't she know that's what he was after?

Isn't that what she wanted?

"So, I came down to talk some sense into her. Rape." He spit on the ground.

The marble floor.

"What did she say?" asked Edwin, barely controlling his urge to punch him.

"Mr. Talki doesn't want a scene, doesn't want publicity, you know. No police. 'It is not so good for the hotel.' So he says, if we both go quietly, it will be best for everyone. Including the Ciragan."

"And she agreed?"

For some reason, he couldn't imagine Adriana agreeing to so tame a resolution.

"Yes, she agreed. I think she was embarrassed. I mean, she knows she is in the wrong."

Edwin bit his tongue. Don't disagree with the terrorist sitting beside you.

Hazzim hit Edwin on the chest in a confidential gesture. He leaned shakily toward him.

"Don't bother with that one, Edwin Sterling."

Edwin uneasily held his breath as Hazzim grabbed hold of his arm and leaned close to his face.

"I know you like her, I can see that. She is beautiful, it is true, but no one deserves to be tasered." He shook his head as if removing the memory of her from his mind. "She is not worth the trouble, my friend. Ahmed! A drink! This tasering thing still makes me feel sick."

34

Edwin parted with Hazzim and company and headed
to his room. It had been a long day. A long, yo-yo
emotional, too much informational day.

Going up the stairs, he couldn't help but look for
his friend, the mustachioed hotel employee. If he was
watching, Edwin did not see him.

Adriana was waiting for him when he got to his
door. She had been watching for him and came down
the hall as he put in the key.

"May I come in?" she asked.

Hazzim. Tasers.

He checked for a handbag. Nothing.

"Just for a minute," she pleaded.

Her eyes scanned the hall for signs of anyone
approaching.

Play your part, Edwin.

The jilted lover.

Who knows nothing about terrorists.

He opened the door and allowed her to pass through.

"Edwin!" she said, trying to put her arms around
him.

He stepped back, pushing her away.

She looked stricken, surprised. She swallowed, but continued.

"I just went through a lot. I need someone to hold me," she explained. She looked exhausted.

Edwin made no move toward her.

"I can explain everything," she said.

He folded his arms and waited.

"Not here," she said. "Not now."

Exasperated, he walked away.

"How many times do I have to hear that?" he asked.

"I asked you to trust me!"

"And I did, Adriana! But you're nothing but a liar. You toyed with my feelings from the start! Admit it! All the way from "let's be friends"!" He laughed derisively. "What was I thinking? I should never have continued our relationship after that. Phillip told me there must be another man. But no! I thought you actually liked me. I thought you were telling me the truth, that it was work that was taking up all your time. I thought there was hope for us."

Once the words started tumbling out, it was difficult for him to stop.

"I've never lied to you." Tears were rolling down her cheeks. "Everything I said to you, everything you thought I felt, was the truth."

"Do you even feel anything? You're kissing me one minute, and throwing yourself into the arms of another man the next! How do you expect me to feel about that? And how is that not lying?" He slammed his fist against the back of the chair he was standing behind.

"You were never supposed to be here!"

"Well, I am here. I witnessed it all. All the sordid details."

He clenched his jaw and gripped the back of the chair.

"So, is this it?" she asked. "Now? Are you saying there's no hope for us?"

"There is no us. I've been a fool to believe there ever was."

She looked at him with so much pain, he almost felt sorry for her. Almost relented.

But not quite.

"I thought you were different, Adriana. I thought we were different." Now the tears streamed down his own face. Tears of pain and self-pity.

She wiped her tears with the back of her hand.

"You put me on a pedestal, Edwin," she said, backing toward the door. "I thought you knew better."

35

The flight from Istanbul was torturous.

He had had another sleepless night. He break-fasted in his room and didn't see Hazzim or Adriana when he came down with his luggage. He assumed they were both already gone.

Mr. Talki was mysteriously solemn, almost stand-offish toward him as he helped him with his luggage.

"I hope you had a pleasant stay at the Ciragan Palace Hotel, Meester Sterling," he said without smiling.

"The hotel was everything it should be," he replied.

A true statement.

The manager packed Edwin into the car. Then he leaned his head in.

"Perhaps you will visit America soon?" he suggested.

Edwin shook his head.

"There's nothing for me in America."

Only pain.

And he did feel pain. He could tell himself all he wanted that he had fallen in love with a wanted criminal, but it didn't erase his feelings. For some reason, they were stubborn, as if they had a will of their own.

The airport in Istanbul was crowded when he had arrived. He had passed a group of French schoolgirls on some kind of class trip. He knew instinctively that they whispered as he passed, watched him, recognized him. Somewhere in the back of his mind, a camera flashed.

In Heathrow, his driver, Bill, met him inside instead of waiting for him at the curb.

"You'd better prepare yourself, Mr. Sterling," he said.

Paparazzi.

How long had he been in Turkey? Five days? It had seemed like a lifetime. Anonymity was only a dream.

"How do they know I'm here?" he asked, putting on his warm coat and scarf. Back to English weather.

"IPhone photograph from the Istanbul airport," said Bill. "They knew you were coming home."

The French schoolgirls.

He popped the collar of his coat up as he stepped outside the airport. With Bill's help, he attempted to push through the crowd of photographers.

"What do you think about Chloe's engagement?"

"You ran away to Istanbul. Was it to heal your broken heart?"

Chloe? Good Lord.

She had become a distant memory.

He brushed them all aside without commenting and collapsed into the car. At home, he crashed into his bed, fully clothed, and didn't wake until morning.

The next day was clear and bright, with an unnaturally blue sky.

It's October, for God's sake. Where's the rain?

There's nothing more irritating than to be depressed on a sunny day.

Saw u r home on the internet please call Mom ;)

The last person in the world he wanted to talk to right then was his mother, but he knew she would worry if he didn't call.

"Edwin, you look terrible," Portia Valentine said as soon as she picked up the phone.

"You can't even see me!"

"On the internet photos. Just awful. Like you haven't slept. By the way, did you see my winky face? Millicent taught me how to do that."

Edwin sighed.

"Anyway, your father and I would like you to come to tea today. You can tell us about your trip. The one you never mentioned you were going on."

"Sorry, Mother. It was spur of the moment. I should never have gone."

"That's what your father says. We'll expect you at 4:00. And Edwin?"

"Yes, Mother?"

"Take a shower."

He did take a shower. A long one. Standing under the streaming hot water, he tried to wash Istanbul from his soul. Crying in the shower doesn't count because your tears wash down the drain. This time there was no one to witness any redness around his eyes.

He called Phillip to let him know he was still alive.

"What happened?" he asked. "Did you notice anything suspicious?"

"It's a long story," Edwin responded wearily. "One that will need to be told face to face at some point."

"I'll definitely need a complete play-by-play. Did you do or say anything, anything at all, that would have caused them to be suspicious of you?"

"Apparently not."

I was the spider's confidante in the end.

"Good. We don't want this following you home. Jeff may want to speak to you. Off the record and all that."

"Yeah. I figured."

"I'm sorry about all this, Ed. I really am. I wish it had turned out differently. But I'm really glad you're okay."

"You tried to warn me. I wouldn't listen."

"It happens to the best of us, mate."

"You know, I really don't think so. How many friends do you know who have fallen in love with a terrorist?"

"Good point. Maybe it only happens to my best friend. But I'm glad he's still alive to tell about it."

"Me, too."

I think.

He really second-guessed that when David called.

"Edwin!" was all he managed to say. Edwin could feel the rage he was holding back in the silence that followed.

"I'm sorry, David. I know this makes me look foolish."

"Let me explain something to you," his publicist said through obviously clenched teeth. "This is not about my job or how much work this makes me have to do to make you look like a hero again. Which I will have to work hard to do!"

"I'm sorry."

"This is not only about your career, which you apparently don't care about. It's about all the careers that ride on yours. Think about it, Edwin. You don't live in a bubble. Your career, your image, affects everyone else around you. And not just me. Think about the show. *Dr. Hanover.* If England hates Edwin Sterling, they hate *Dr. Hanover.* If the show tanks, it takes everyone down with it. Genevieve, Harry, the producers, the writers. You can't let your personal life rule your career! Think, Edwin. Get yourself together!"

Edwin was stunned. And ashamed.

"It won't happen again, David," he promised. "I'll get myself together."

Edwin was at his parents' house promptly at four.

In the cab ride over, he had received a text from Chloe.

Didnt know u were so heartbroken. Call me! Im not married yet.

Good Lord! This is all I need.

As soon as he walked in the door, his mother embraced him. It was a long embrace, as if she knew the danger he had been in and was relieved he had made it through.

But she couldn't know.

"Darling," she said, patting his cheek. "You look tired."

Even his father hugged him instead of his usual handshake.

It's only been about a week since I've seen them.

Odd.

They had tea and chatted about inconsequential

things. Edwin tried to play the part of the dutiful son, feigning interest in the trivial matters of his mother's latest role in a play or the neighbor's daughter's marriage. It all seemed so mundane, so unimportant.

So safe.

He had a sudden revelation, sitting there in his parents' rose-covered sitting room.

He liked being in grave danger. He liked that there was no other kind. It made him feel alive, maybe even needed, definitely real.

"Edwin? You're doing it again," said his mother.

"What?"

"That faraway look thing. I don't think you heard what I said."

"I'm sorry, Mother. I've got a lot on my mind."

"Adriana, eh?" asked Sir Thomas, nodding.

Edwin agreed, surprised.

"I wish you'd told me you found out where she was," said his father. "I would have advised you not to go."

"I wouldn't have listened," Edwin admitted.

"Well, if I were you, I wouldn't have listened to me, either."

"I'm just glad you're safe," said his mother, patting his leg.

"How much did Phillip tell you?" he asked.

"Oh, sweetheart, Phillip doesn't know much.

He just told us that he'd found a photograph of Adriana with Hazzim Nejem, and you'd gone off to confront her."

"A reckless move," said his father. "Completely unaccounted for. You surprised quite a few people. But it all worked out all right."

Edwin stared dumbfoundedly at his father.

"It all worked out?" he repeated, irritated.

"Well, yes. Didn't she tell you? The mission was a success."

"What are you talking about?" asked Edwin.

His parents exchanged surprised glances.

"You mean, Adriana didn't tell you?" asked his mother.

"Tell me what?"

"Who she really is."

"Oh, I know who she really is, all right," he said sarcastically. "The real Adriana. Her actions spoke loud and clear."

"Oh dear," said his mother, her hand on her heart. "I can't believe I have been so remiss. How I raised a son, under my own melodramatic roof, who can't recognize an actress when he sees one. Love truly must be blind."

An actress?

An actress.

His mother grabbed his hand.

"Darling, this may come as a surprise to you, but..."

She looked to her husband to finish her sentence.

"Son, Adriana works for the CIA."

What color was left in Edwin's face turned ashen.

What have I done?

"We thought she would have told you, now that it's all over."

"She didn't get a chance," said Edwin. "I wouldn't listen."

Scenes flew through Edwin's mind in an instant. He could hear her voice.

In Kensington: "I have to concentrate on work right now. I can't be distracted by—by anything."

At his birthday: "There are things I have to do. You won't be able to get in touch with me for awhile."

In Istanbul: "You shouldn't be here. I don't want you to get hurt."

She'd been trying to tell him. But she couldn't tell him. And he wouldn't listen. He heard what he wanted to hear, always hearing it selfishly. Always self-pity, thinking she was pushing him away. But she was trying to protect him. She wasn't concerned about hurting him emotionally, she was afraid for his life. And he stubbornly stayed, and then stubbornly left.

He rubbed his forehead with his hand.

"We're stressing him," his mother said to his father.

"He always does that when he's stressed."

"It was a stressful business," his father agreed. "But we got the information we needed to link Hazzim to the attempts on Tastan. Thanks to Adriana."

Edwin looked suspiciously at his father.

"Why do you know all this?"

"What do you think your father has been doing in the government all these years?" his mother asked.

"Making policy? Sitting on committees?" Edwin offered weakly.

"Oh tush. That's boring."

"Part of making foreign policy is protecting our interests abroad," said Sir Thomas. "We can't have a Turkish oil magnate being killed off, especially on British soil. Especially when he wants to make us a deal. We had information that there would be an attempt on Tastan's life while he was here. Adriana was essential in keeping that from happening."

"My head's going to explode."

"Oh, don't be ridiculous, Edwin," scolded his mother. "Heads don't explode half so often as people say."

"Why would an American—spy—help us?"

"Mutually beneficial," Sir Thomas explained. "We were all together in this one. America, England, Turkey. Adriana has an expertise in Turkish relations, because of her background. I didn't know who she was, at first. I knew someone was in the country. When she disarmed your crazy fan, it became clear to me. That's why I insisted she come over for dinner."

"That's why you were acting so odd," said Edwin.

"So, with Adriana's expertise, she was the one sent to cozy up to Hazzim so she could get what we needed."

"What did we need?"

"Proof. We knew Hazzim was responsible for the plane crash in the Balkans, and we knew he wanted the last son dead, but we couldn't prove it. Couldn't link him to it. He was very clever."

Edwin nodded. The spider is definitely devious.

"So you knew he was a terrorist, but you needed proof."

"Hazzim's no terrorist."

"But I thought it was terrorists who were after Mr. Tastan? I thought the other Muslim nations were angry with Kara Inci!"

"Oh, they're angry all right," said his father. "No denying it. But they aren't trying to kill him. No, Hazzim has a personal vendetta. Kara Inci is hurting the BOC bank account. The playboy may have to actually get a job."

"He only made it look like terrorism," said his mother. "A red herring, so to speak."

Edwin considered his mother, all smiling and matronly, pouring tea and speaking of terrorism as if it were perfectly normal.

He closed his eyes.

I will open them, and it will all have been a dream. Because this can't be reality.

He opened his eyes, but the scene was the same. His mother, piddling with the tea things. His father studying him in an odd way, pulling on his chin.

My father is somehow part of British Intelligence.

My mother knows it.

And the woman I love is a spy.

Who thinks I hate her.

"I have to go," he said suddenly, getting up from the sofa.

"Where are you going?" his mother asked, concerned.

"I don't know," Edwin answered, running his hands through his hair and standing his curls on end. "I have to find her. It didn't end well."

"She shouldn't be hard to find," said Sir Thomas. "She had a briefing this morning."

"She's in England?"

"She was this morning."

His mother grabbed his hand.

"She loves you, Edwin."

"I wish I had your confidence," he said, kissing her forehead. "You wouldn't be proud of the way I handled myself."

36

Edwin Sterling, you fool.

You selfish fool.

He sat in the back of a cab, headed to Bethany's house. It was the first place he thought of to check.

Adriana a spy. Always trying to prevent a death, not cause one.

"I've never lied to you, Edwin."

She was telling the truth. She may not have told him everything, but she never lied.

Please God, let me find her. And make her listen.

His phone buzzed in his pocket. It was Jen, reminding him that a decision needed to be made on the script he was considering.

Play your part, Edwin.

That won't do, anymore. Merely playing a part.

I want reality.

As he stared down at his phone, an idea occurred to him.

He opened the Find My Friends app.

Adriana locating.

Come on, hurry.

Adriana Found.

He frantically watched the map as it began to pin-point her location.

"Turn around!" he called to the cabbie.

I know exactly where she is.

Edwin alighted at the corner. He had to push through a group of tourists lined up to get on a dou-ble-decker tour bus.

"That was Edwin Sterling!" someone called after him, but he didn't stop.

The evening, although still sunny, was becoming colder.

It is October, after all.

Edwin was glad he had remembered to wear his coat, but he had no hat. His curls, recognizable even by the most casual of fans, were blowing around his face as he walked. He could feel eyes upon him, watching him, following him.

Look straight ahead. Don't look them in the eye. Finding Adriana is all that matters.

It's a matter of life and death.

He had said those very words hundreds of times as Dr. Hanover.

"*It's a matter of life and death.*"

But it was meaningless, playing a part. Now he had actually experienced it. Grave danger, sitting beside a man who could slap his arm in friendship one moment and order his death the next.

"Aren't you Edwin Sterling?"

Edwin shook his head, swerving to avoid the speaker, an eager young woman with a pack of enamored friends gawking behind her, awaiting his response.

"Not today!" he said, leaving her stunned on the sidewalk. "It's a matter of life and death!"

Finding Adriana is a matter of life and death.

I accused her of being a liar, when all the while she was just playing a part to save a man's life. Life and death. This is life and death, because life without her is death.

Edwin began to run.

He ran down the Broad Walk, past the mothers with children, past the tourists, past the dog walkers, past the undercover guards pretending to be joggers.

He ran past Victoria's statue.

"Wish me luck," he said to her as he passed.

He wound through the Wiggly Walk, through to the Cradle Walk and the Sunken Garden. When he finally reached the entrance, he paused to catch his breath.

It was shadowy under the lime trees. Edwin could see the bench, their bench, from where he stood.

It was empty.

He took a deep breath, a calming breath, and went on.

Maybe she's around the corner.

He walked the length of the first corridor of the arbor, but his steps slowed as he approached the corner.

What if she never wants to see me again? I wouldn't blame her.

But then, she wouldn't have come here.

He stepped boldly around the corner.

And there she stood.

Framed in the archway that overlooked the garden.

She turned her head quickly when she saw him. She had been crying.

They faced each other, neither of them knowing what to do or what to say.

She was first to break the silence.

"How did you find me?" she asked.

He shrugged.

"Find my Friends."

She smiled, despite her tears.

"I thought I'd never see you again," she admitted. "I came here to say goodbye—to us."

"Don't give up on us yet," he said, stepping closer.

"You said there was no us. That there never was."

"I lied."

He cupped her face in his hands and kissed her gently.

"Adriana, I haven't been a good friend to you."

"It was a lot to ask. Too much to ask," she said.

She broke down then, covering her face with her hands. He gave her his handkerchief and held her in his arms. She pressed her face against his chest.

"Why didn't you just tell me?" he whispered.

"And put you in further danger? No. I needed you to leave Istanbul, alive. It was my fault you were involved at all. I should never have—but for the first time in my life, I found someone who liked me, the real me. Who wasn't intimidated by my intelligence, or impressed by my family. And you were just so—wonderful!"

"I think you've got the wrong man," he said, wiping her face. "I haven't shown myself to be very wonderful lately."

"You're wrong, Edwin. You came after me. You shouldn't have done it, but you came after me. What girl can resist a man who sees her in a photograph and travels to Istanbul to find her? You almost killed the mission, but you were wonderful."

Flashes. Reporters.

"Edwin! Is this your response to Chloe's engagement? Another woman?"

"That's the Mystery Woman! Edwin! Edwin, is that the Mystery Woman?"

Shouts inside the Cradle Walk as reporters and cameras approached them.

Edwin shielded Adriana's face from the cameras.

Jostling. Pressing.

No privacy. No respect.

Suddenly, a dark-haired man came from behind Edwin and began shooing the paparazzi out of the Cradle Walk. Out on the lawn, he noticed official-looking people moving the gathering crowd of fans and onlookers.

I guess Edwin Sterling running through Kensington Park shouting, "It's a matter of life and death," attracts a little bit of attention.

Sorry David.

It would be easy for the crowd to assume that the gentlemen were part of Edwin's bodyguard, or some kind of security detail, but Edwin knew it was CIA or MI6 or some sort of—

He paused in his thoughts as he recognized the man who had been removing the paparazzi. The man gave Edwin his signature sneering smile, only this time he raised two fingers to his eyebrow in a salute. He wasn't wearing his uniform, but he was unmistakably the sinister hotel employee from the Ciragan.

"Thank you," Edwin said.

He turned his attention back to Adriana.

"I've just realized today that I'm guilty of doing the very things I said I hated," he said to her, thoughtfully. "David proved to me that I was selfish, that

I wasn't thinking of others, only myself. And you accused me of putting you on a pedestal," he said, remembering their last encounter in Istanbul. "You were right. And I should have known better, like you said. It's what I've always hated about this fame thing. False expectations. I tried to make you perfect, and when I thought—"

"I'm so sorry I couldn't tell you, that I had to make you think I was some kind of—"

He shook his head.

"I should have trusted you. You asked me to, and I said I would. But you're right. You fell off my pedestal."

"What should we do about it?" she asked, looking up into his face. He smiled down at her.

"The pedestal? Let's destroy it."

37

They sat in the sitting room of Edwin's parents' home. Millicent had brought in coffee and retired from the room.

Edwin and Adriana sat on the sofa, holding hands.

I'm never letting go again.

"A job well done, Adriana," Sir Thomas said, nodding in her direction.

"Yes, bravo," agreed Edwin's mother.

"Just got word that Hazzim is in custody," Sir Thomas announced. "And we were able to catch quite a few of his colleagues, as well."

Adriana smiled. "That's good news."

"Mr. Tastan sends his personal gratitude. He says he's looking forward to meeting such a brave young lady."

Adriana blushed.

"So you really haven't met him?" Edwin said, bewildered.

"Not officially, no," she replied.

"What's this I hear of you retiring?" asked Portia Valentine.

"Well," she explained, "not retiring. But moving out of field work. I entered the CIA when I had nothing to live for."

She looked shyly at Edwin.

"Nothing to live for?" declared his mother.

"I've never had a normal life," Adriana explained. "My father was an American, but my mother was Turkish. Her family came to America in the 1920's." She looked at Sir Thomas. "After the fall of the Ottoman Empire."

"I thought I recognized a family resemblance," he said.

"My mother was part of the extended family of the Osmans, the Ottomans. We were sent into exile after they established the Republic of Turkey. The Sultan was one of my grandfather's cousins. We are spread out now: Europe, the Middle East, America. We've recently been allowed back into the country again. But it's bittersweet. What's gone is gone."

"So, you're a princess?" asked Edwin.

She laughed. "Sort of, I guess. But so much was lost in those wars, for Turkey, for my family, for history. And so much has been gained. In my own line of the family, it's a complete change from what used to be because my mother became a Christian when she married my father. So, I grew up very American, very privileged, I guess you could say.

My father's business was successful, I went to the best schools. But there was always that tension of East and West. I had Muslim grandparents on one side and Christian grandparents on the other. I became interested in history because of that. And the Middle East became a special interest for me, for obvious reasons. I really am an historian," she added.

"Good to know."

"I thought academia would be my life. A nice, quiet museum, or professorship somewhere, where I could study and teach. Where I could talk about the wars and the tension but not have to be involved in them. And then my parents were killed in a plane crash. It was my father's plane. They were flying to New York. The loss was incredible, so much more than I expected."

"I'm so sorry, my dear," said Portia Valentine, compassionately.

"My brother was there for a time, but his life was already so much more. He's a Marine. Special forces. Saving the world, and all that. He had never been afraid to fight for what he believed in. I felt like my life was meaningless, that I wasn't doing anything. And I no longer had anything to live for. If I died, I mean. Nobody I would be leaving behind. Except my brother, but I knew he'd be okay."

Edwin shifted uneasily. He hated to hear her say those words.

Her life would have mattered to me. It does matter to me. If she'd been reckless—he pushed that thought away.

"I'd already been approached by CIA recruiters, during college," Adriana continued, "partly because of my brother, partly because of my mother's family and my knowledge of Turkey, my ease with the language. I turned them down the first time. My family life was enough turmoil for me. This time, I said yes."

"Enter Edwin Sterling, crasher of missions," said Edwin.

Everyone laughed.

"Enter Edwin Sterling, stealer of hearts," she said. "You were so unexpected. All the way to the end, unexpected. Muhammed was so frustrated with you."

"Muhammed?"

"At the hotel. The one who put a knife to your throat."

"Oh! My mustachioed friend."

"On our side, of course. Turkish intelligence. I told you he was protecting me from you. That's why he was in my room, to argue about you. He wanted you gone. He didn't trust you."

"I am exactly who I say I am."

"It was true. Of course, after that, he was there for your protection, also. Unwillingly."

Edwin's mind went back to the Ciragan. *Protecting me, not trying to intimidate me. Or maybe both.*

"So, back to the beginning," he said. "I'm still confused about this whole mission thing. You came to England to protect Mr. Tastan?"

"Yes. We had intelligence that there would be an attempt on his life during his speech, and we knew it would be a shooter because we knew who had been hired. We had Bethany in the catwalk waiting. She was able to shoot the would-be assassin before he accomplished his purpose."

"Bethany?" Edwin exclaimed.

"Yes. She's CIA, too."

"Bethany?"

"Why are you so surprised?"

"She doesn't look anything like what I would expect a secret agent to look like."

"Really, Edwin," complained his mother. "This isn't James Bond!"

"She's right," agreed Adriana. "You want someone to blend in, not stick out. She may not look like a Bond Girl, but Bethany was a champion sharpshooter in college. I'll take Bethany over James Bond any day!"

"Hear, hear," said Sir Thomas.

She really is a predatory bird.

"Bethany was really uneasy about you. She didn't want me to go out with you because she felt it was putting the mission at risk. All the paparazzi and the publicity. She was right."

"And the second attempt?" asked Edwin.

"We weren't sure how it would happen, but we were tight on security at the flat. That's the reason I used visiting Kensington as an alibi; it was nearby."

"So I was a decoy."

"You were conveniently hospitable. And it gave me more time with you. I was selfish, too," she admitted, squeezing his hand. "Then the crazy fan almost blew my cover. I had to defend myself. The constable wasn't convinced I had learned self-defense watching my brother's karate class."

"No," agreed Edwin.

"I actually did. At first. But I had more training later."

"And that's when I knew who you were," said Sir Thomas.

"So she really was just a crazy fan?" asked Edwin. "No spy stuff?"

"No spy stuff, but Bethany was furious that it was all over the news."

"I can imagine."

"So with two attempts thwarted, we knew Hazzim

would try again. He had been in Ibiza the whole time. Mr. Tastan left Britain for Turkey. He was safe for now. Hazzim was back at square one. He had expected one of his two attempts to succeed. He had to come up with a new plan and give himself some space so as not to attract attention. We monitored him for three months. When he moved himself into Turkey, we knew things were beginning to move again. That's why I went there."

"That's why you were able to come to my birthday party?"

"Yes. There was just enough time before I needed to be in Istanbul. I insisted on going. Bethany, again, wasn't happy about it. She felt it was a waste of time. And your father wasn't happy about it, either."

Sir Thomas agreed. "It was a dangerous move that could have put the mission at risk," he said sternly.

She bowed her head. "I know. But it was so important to Edwin that I be there," she said to Sir Thomas.

She turned to Edwin. "And I wanted to see you. I was afraid—"

"Of what?"

"Of something going wrong. I was afraid I'd never see you again."

It was a matter of life and death.

"Well, *I'm* glad you came, my dear," said Edwin's mother, trying to lighten the mood.

"In Istanbul, I was monitoring his actions, his friends, his meetings with people. With Mr. Tastan's American trip coming up, we knew those would be the target dates."

"What we wanted was to arrest Hazzim before-hand, but we needed the evidence to link him to the first attempts," Sir Thomas added. "He was very care-ful to throw suspicion on terrorist groups and to keep himself from being directly linked."

"What evidence were you looking for?" asked Edwin.

"Hazzim had a Dayrunner," he explained, "a per-sonal planner with all his meetings and contacts. He used that instead of anything digital so that it couldn't be traced. He kept it with him at all times."

"My job was to get close enough to take a few photographs of the pages without him knowing," explained Adriana. "To show his contacts, his meetings."

"That's why you were flirting with him. I feel like such a fool."

"Such a romantic fool!" she teased. "In the rose garden, when you told me not to have anything to do with him, I was so afraid you had figured out what I was doing. Your safety was always a concern. At any moment you could have said something or done something that would have blown the whole thing and put us all in danger."

"Like mentioning Mr. Tastan to Hazzim?"

"Yes! Like that. But you were afraid I was walking into the arms of a womanizer. You were coming to my rescue. I was so—honored."

"What happened in his suite? Did you really taser him? He told me his side of the story."

Edwin clenched his fist, remembering.

"I'm surprised!" she said. "He was so jealous of you. We knew the preparations had been laid for another attempt on Mr. Tastan. He had had two meetings with Turkish hit men, people who could accompany Mr. Tastan as 'security' but would actually be his assassins. One in Troy, you remember. The other while we were in the Spice Bazaar. My signal to go ahead was the blue bath salts."

"What?"

"Pink would have meant abort. My contact suggested blue, so I knew that was the night. The plan was moving forward. We had dinner. I had convinced him that he had won me over, that he would be able to finally have his way with me. When he tried, he really did get aggressive. I pushed him off, grabbed the taser out of my purse, and let him have it."

"And it knocked him unconscious?"

"No. Tasers only incapacitate. He was conscious, although he was disoriented and in pain. It was the propofol I injected in him that knocked him out. It works for about five minutes. Long enough for me to get what I needed. Then I just waited until he was coming to, and stood over him accusing him of rape."

"Wow. And he never knew."

"No.   Hazzim would never suspect a stupid American woman of getting the best of him. Which is a good thing," she added, seriously.

"Yes, a very good thing," agreed Sir Thomas.

"So it was all a show. It felt like it, when I was watching it unfold."

"Yes, a show, so to speak. I made a big production of accusing him of rape. I was able to slip Mr. Talki the disk I had, and his solution for resolving the problem was for both of us to leave."

"Mr. Talki?" asked Edwin, incredulous.

"Of course, Mr. Talki," Adriana said. "He was my primary contact in Turkey."

"So he wasn't just an old romantic."

"Well," she said, "he really is. He liked you from the start. He warned me not to lose you."

"I knew I liked Mr. Talki," said Edwin.

"Which brings us here," said his father, winking.

"Yes, it does," Adriana agreed, looking at Edwin.

"You know, Thomas, we really ought to feed these two. We haven't had a bite since tea."

"You are right, my dear," Sir Thomas agreed.

All four rose from their seats.

"No, no, dear," Edwin's mother said, waving them off. "We'll see to it."

Edwin's parents exited the room. His mother closed the mahogany pocket doors behind her.

Edwin turned toward Adriana, taking her in his arms.

He leaned his forehead against hers.

"This may not be a rose garden," he said, glancing around the room, "but it does have rose wallpaper."

Adriana laughed.

A happy, contented, truthful laugh.

"You said you had nothing to live for. That's why you joined the CIA."

"It's true."

"And you want out now?"

"I found something to live for."

"He told me what happened, you know," said Edwin. "Hazzim. Warned me against you. Said you weren't worth my time."

"What do you think? Is he right?" she asked, her lips dangerously close to his.

"I think you're the best thing that's ever happened to me."

"Never stop saying that!" she whispered, smiling.

"No more Hazzim?" he asked.

"No more Hazzim."

"No more pedestals?"
"No more pedestals."
"Just us?"
She kissed him.
No more playing a part.
This is real.

THE END